I0520396

"Doctor, now I'm seeing things," I complained to Dr. Chopra.

"What kinds of things?"

"It's hard to explain. I see things before they happen. Not very far in advance, only a few seconds or a minute at most. Especially in mirrors. It's as though I catch a glimpse of something that isn't reflected from anywhere, just like when you gave me that pen test. But then it always arrives a second or two later, just as I saw it in the reflection."

"Well." Dr. Chopra considered this. "Would you like to try the mirror test again?"

"Yes."

He set it up, just as before, first placing a pen behind me while he held the mirror in front, then to each side of me. I had no trouble, on this occasion, reaching for the pen opposite each reflection.

Then something strange happened.

Quite clearly, I saw Dr. Chopra's assistant walking down the hall and open the door to his office. The angle was quite odd, as if it were only a reflection *but I did not see it in the mirror.*

(from *Refractions from the Neglected Side*)

ALSO BY TARA MAYA

THE PAINTED WORLD, STORIES, VOL. 1
TOMORROW WE DANCE

THE WINDWHEEL AND THE MAZE SERIES:
(2011)

THE UNFINISHED SONG
THE KIVA BENEATH THE WORLD
THE NIGHT RAINBOW

CONMERGENCE
AN ANTHOLOGY OF SPECULATIVE FICTION

TARA MAYA

MISQUE PRESS

Copyright © 2010 by Tara Maya
Cover Design by Tara Maya

All rights reserved. Except as permitted under the U.S. Copyright Act of
1976, no part of this publication may be reproduced, distributed, or
transmitted in any form or by any means, or stored in a database or retrieval
system, without the prior written permission of the publisher

Misque
Misque Press

First North American Edition: October 2010.

The characters and events in this book are fictitious. Any similarity to real
persons, living or dead, is coincidental and not intended by the author.

ISBN: 0983107300
9780983107309

In memory of my grandmama
who taught me to read,
and to love books.
But not to cook.

Acknowledgements

Hugs for my mom, kisses for my husband and gooby kisses for my kids. Big thank-yous to so many others: to all the members of the On-line Writing Workshop; to my many other internet writing buddies; to all of you who read and/or comment on my blog; to Michelle Davidson Argyle and Domey Malasarn of The Literary Lab; to Zoe Winters; and to my wonderful editor who knows, among other things, the proper terminology for matters neurological, Kathleen Gresham.

CONTENTS

Introduction

Ten years ago, I ran away from home. I didn't actually sleep on the streets when I was homeless. I never made a little newspaper tent or pushed around a shopping cart. If I had no place to flop for the night, I would be too scared to sleep, so I would stay awake all night, ride buses, or hang out under the single yellow light bulb over the back entrance to the public library, as if I just had a book that was urgently overdue and required me to wait all night to return it the very second the library opened at 10 am. Sometimes I stayed at homeless shelters. Mostly I crashed with friends.

Kids run away from home for many good reasons, but I wasn't a kid, and my reason was ludicrous. True, my mom and I had a fundamental disagreement. I wanted to write novels for a living, and I was prepared to do whatever I needed to do to achieve my dream, especially if it involved sponging off my mom and writing all day on a glass veranda that opened onto a swimming pool. My mom thought I should stop being such a frickin' mooch, go get a real job and write as a hobby, like a sane human being. She warned me that if I tried to have a career as a writer, I would probably just end up homeless and penniless, living on the streets. She convinced me to leverage my BA into a credential to do substitute teaching. Every morning, around five AM, I dragged myself to the phone. If it rang, it meant I had to drive to some junior high school and sit through a melee of pubescent mayhem while I wrote by hand in my notebook. If the phone didn't ring, it meant I could stay home and write on a computer by the backyard pool. Sometimes at 4:56, I took the phone off the hook.

My mom nagged me to earn a Master's in Education, so I could enjoy pubescent hormones as a steady career. I'm not good at saying no to my mom, so I kept promising to think about it, all the while secretly promising myself I would publish a breakout novel instead, something that would earn enough money I would be justified in writing full time. I knew it would be hard because in junior high and high school, I'd already written several novels, all awful. Then, in my late teens, I spent another five years writing a 400,000 word fantasy epic, *The Games of Dragon Island: Book One of Avatars of the Archons*, which I submitted to DAW when I was nineteen. I didn't know anything about agents. Writing wasn't a business to me; it wasn't even an art. It was just an after-effect of being alive. You were alive, so you wrote. If you stopped writing, you would die, and also, the sun would probably go out because you hadn't sacrificed your heart to it.

Peter Stampfel returned my doorstop to me with a nice personalized rejection, saying thanks but they weren't publishing any books with reincarnation at the moment, there were too many *Wheel of Time* imitators. Again, I was too green to realize how kind it was of him to write me a personal note. (So Peter, on the off chance you ever read this: You rock. And your banjo music rocks. Thanks.) That same year, I didn't get into college because my grades in high school sucked. Let's agree it was a despondent moment and move on.

I did three things. I bummed around Europe for a while, on the pretext of learning French. I attended a Junior College for a semester, earned a 4.0, reapplied to my dream college, and this time was accepted. I also bought the first book in the *Wheel of Time* series, which I had never read, to see why Peter Stampfel thought my book was imitating it. I didn't think my book was at all similar, but I did enjoy the book and then the series. There are worse writers to be compared to than Robert Jordan.

I managed to concentrate enough on college to graduate and only once came close to flunking because I was inspired to write a book during finals. I earned better grades than I did in high school, thanks to the notable absence of math in my curriculum. But college only lasts four, or, um, five years, and then you have to either move on and Become An Adult or else hang around your mom's house a few more years, *pretending* to be an adult.

The more my mother urged me to become a teacher, the more determined I was that I had to become a professional writer, not just someone who wrote for fun. I learned all about agents, queries, royalties, advances. I began to panic about how long it would take to get published and earn real money at it. I felt guiltier and guiltier that I wasn't working at a real job. Whole days started to go by where I stared at my computer screen, or class full of rowdy students, and wrote nothing. My mind was frozen. The sun had gone out.

I blamed my mom.

I knew what would happen. I would give in to the voice of reason and common sense and become a teacher. At first, I would write in the evenings, but gradually, work would overwhelm me or drain me. Queries would be sent and rejected. My inspiration would flag. I'd become depressed and self-doubting. I'd say I would write as soon as I had time. But I would have less and less time. The years would go by, and occasionally I would fiddle with my novel, or dash out a short story. But mostly I would just write the stories in my head and never have the chance to polish them.

I decided I would rather be homeless and penniless but free to write than to subside into suburban catatonia. I had no money, no car, no career, no house, no plan. Just a dream.

So I ran away from home to become a writer.

And yeah, ended up homeless and penniless and living on the streets. So it turns out my mom was right all along.

Several of these stories have had previous homes in small, mostly free, mostly online magazines. A few extracts from novels have put on Groucho Marx glasses and sneaked in masquerading as novelettes. They have never before been published. However, even the stories that were published are no longer available or are difficult to track down. Honestly, some I myself had even forgotten about until I decided to compile this anthology.

I ask all readers to let me know if you find any typos or mistakes, so I can improve future editions.

GHOSTS ON RED STRINGS

FOR FIFTEEN YEARS, Osok lived next to the man who had raped her and killed her children.

Because the banana trees grew so tall, she could not see his house from her porch, though his house, like hers, stood high on stilts. When she could, she pretended his house was not there.

Today, while she was pounding yams under her house, he passed by on his bicycle. As he was one of the few people in the village with a bicycle, he was very proud of it. He paused in front of her house. He climbed off his bicycle, left it leaning against a tree and approached her.

"Good day, Nabu Osok," he said with a big grin.

Her stomach knotted. She hated his smile. *What does he have to smile about?* she wondered. She did not smile back.

"Good day, Wabu Wayook," she said.

"Fine sky today, isn't it?"

"It is a sunny day."

"How are your children?" he asked politely. He did not mean, of course, the ones he had murdered. He meant the three sons she and her new husband had together.

"They are fine," Osok said. "Fishing, with their father. I hear you are to take a new bride."

"Yes." He flushed, puffing up a little. "From another village—from Kalu. She is very young, but she says she loves me."

Osok grunted. She pounded her pestle in her mortar with hard, loud strokes. It was a big, stone pestle, and she imagined smashing in his head with it.

"I didn't see you in the market today," he remarked. "Don't you want to buy some bananas?"

All the banana trees dividing their houses belonged to him.

"Maybe one or two," she said. "But I have nothing to give you in return."

"I want nothing."

He went back to his bicycle to take some bananas out of the basket in the back. Osok stared at him, her heart pounding in time with the rhythm of her pestle. Trailing after Wabu Wayook were two tiny ghosts.

They were the ghosts of her children. Each of them had been tied to him by a string for the past fifteen years, ever since he had hacked off their arms, legs and heads with his banana tree ax. Sometimes they appeared like that, limbless and bleeding, horrible to behold. Sometimes she wanted to scream when she saw them. Today, however, they looked just as they had when they had been alive.

Her little boy, Tutut, was five. He held a toy boat in his hands, one his wabu, his father, had made for him. Tutut's father had been killed fifteen years ago too, but not by Wayook. Therefore, Wayook did not have the string to the ghost of Tutut's father. Wabu Bok, who lived across town and mended fishing nets, had that string.

Her little girl, Lumu, was only three. Her eyes were big in her small brown face. Whenever she saw Osok, she strained against the red string, holding out her arms to her nabu. Tears spilled down her round cheeks. Sometimes in the night, Osok could hear her baby girl crying from next door, crying for her mother to take her back from Wayook, the murderer, crying to take her home. Today, Lumu was mute, but her eyes pleaded all the same.

Nabu, Nabu. Take me home. Don't leave me tied to him.

Wayook returned with a few bananas.

"I am ashamed of such ugly bananas," he said.

"They are fine, ripe and yellow. I have nothing to give you for such fine bananas."

"I ask nothing."

Osok did not bother to gesture to the two yams she had set aside. She knew he had seen them. "Take some yams at least."

"It is not necessary."

"You will shame me before the ghosts," she said. It was just a phrase, just something people said while bargaining, but Osok was aware of the ghosts watching her as she spoke. They were not the ghosts of her ancestors, as the phrase intended, not ghosts at peace who could bring her fortune. These were ghosts who had seen her shamed before they died. Yes, their deaths had not spared them even that, for Wayook had raped her before he hacked up Tutut and Lumu. He and Bok and the others had made her lift her skirt right in front of her husband and children. Her husband had gone mad then and fought them like a wounded boar. Bok had thrust a fishing spear into her husband's stomach. At that very moment, Wayook had thrust himself into her, and she had envied her husband.

"Very well, if you have any yams," shrugged Wayook.

"Take these, though they not are not so ripe and fine as your bananas," Osok urged, handing him the yams. She returned her attention to her mortar and pestle.

He took the yams. He did not leave. He stood there grinning nervously. Wayook played with the red strings tied around his left wrist, the strings to her two ghosts.

"Nabu Osok," he whispered, "Is there anything else you want to trade?"

She knew what he wanted. He wanted to give her back her ghosts. They were her kin; only she could put them to rest. More than anything, she wanted to take her children back in her arms, burn coconut oil for them, and let them know peace. But there was only one way to redeem the ghosts from a murderer; she must forgive him.

She avoided his eyes so he would not see the hate there. Never. Never would she forgive him for what he and his kind had done to her and her family and her people. The new queen, in her far away capital where everyone had bicycles, might say that the Day of Blood was over and it was time for peace. But the new queen's peace did not bring the dead back to life. Osok pissed on such a peace.

Maybe she had to live next to a rapist and murderer. Maybe she had to buy bananas from him. Maybe she had to watch him grin his stupid grin at her each morning as he passed on his fancy bicycle. But she did not have to forgive him. Ever. That was her one justice.

Lumu began to wail. Tutut put his arm around his young sister. The two little ghosts huddled together.

"No, Wabu Wayook, there is nothing else I want to trade," said Osok.

Wayook forced a grin. "Good day to you, Nabu Osok."

"Good day."

Wayook walked back to his bicycle. Tutut and Lumu trailed after him forlornly.

The two ghosts tied to Osok by red strings, Wayook's former wife and daughter—whom Osok had bludgeoned to death fifteen years ago with the very pestle she now used to pound yams—sadly watched him peddle back to his house behind the shroud of banana trees.

Comments on

"Ghosts on Red Strings"

My priority when I was homeless was naturally to find a good writing group. Oh, yeah, and get a job. The thing I had run away from home to avoid. *Ah, sweet irony of life, at last I've found you!* I found a job as a counselor at a homeless shelter for runaways. (And here you thought homelessness was a bad career move.) It was pretty funny, actually. One week I shared a bunk bed with another homeless girl. The next week, I was in charge of giving her blankets.

Which reminds me of a story I heard as a kid. In the Middle Ages, there was a Jewish man who lost his house in a pogrom. He gathered what remained of his belongings and boarded a ship to Spain, but the ship was caught in a storm. He managed to survive and clawed his way to shore. He had lost everything he had ever owned, even the clothes on his back. But he found a Jewish community and found a job teaching Hebrew. He soon had a house, a wife, and a library. The moral of the story, my mother told me, was that they can take everything from you except your education. No one can take away what's in your brain. I've written some sf stories in which they can take that away too, but anyway, for me, even in the sci-fi-ish sounding year of 2000, my brain was safe. I had a college education and I wasn't on crack, so I had a job.

It was a great job, too. I met arsonists and rapists and one serial killer (that I know of). Lots of inspiration for a writer! I worked the night shift, and while the clients were either asleep or setting fires in the corner of the dorm room, I used the work computer to write and surf the net. That's how I found the Del Rey Online Writing Workshop, which back then was free. (It's not run by Del Rey anymore, and it's not free, but as of this writing, it's still reasonable and still great: sff (dot) onlinewritingworkshop (dot) com.)

You may be wondering what any of this has to do with *Ghosts on Red Strings*. Well, eventually, I left the homeless shelter to go be a peace activist in a war-torn country, but I remained a member of OWW. And while being a human shield, I wrote *Ghosts on Red Strings*. I posted it to the workshop, went off to do human-shieldy things, and when I was able to sit again at a computer, I discovered my story had been chosen as the Editor's Choice of the month and won all sorts of blush-inducing remarks from writers and editors I really admired, like Charles Coleman Finlay and Deanna Hoak.

I had almost no time to work on my novel while I was doing human rights work overseas. I wrote a few short stories. I also kept a journal, which annoyed some of my fellow volunteers. I liked to sit on a pillow on the balcony of our shared house, at level with the tree where leaf-cutter ants were building sticky leaf-ball homes for themselves, two or three balls to a tree, each one about the size of a person's head. My teammates preferred to smoke downstairs, below the balcony. Once, while I was typing away, click-click-click, on my laptop, they began talking loudly so I would hear.

"What *does* she write all the time?"

"She's probably writing a tell-all about us."

Without looking up from my screen, I shouted, "So you better be nice to me!"

They were right, of course. I did write a book about them, or rather, about my year as a peace worker, based on my journal notes. A year after I left, the book was on its way to publication. However, there were problems with the small press that was due to publish it, and it never came out.

Ghosts on Red Strings suffered a sad fate as well. Shortly after *Ghosts on Red Strings* was Editor's Choice on the writing workshop, I had an offer to publish the story, but I wasn't able to respond right away, and then September 11 happened, and I had other things on my mind. So I lost that opportunity, which I have always regretted. As a result, the story has never been published before, though it remained dear to me. I am happy to finally publish it here.

CONMERGENCE

ALTHOUGH REGGIE HAD HEARD on CNN that the Phasic Warning Level was up to Orange, he didn't put much stock in that Home Dimension Security crap, and the sight of the armed man walking outside of Starbucks took him by surprise. The man wore a uniform of some sort, dingy, with a silly, squashed cap, and he carried a large automatic. On his chest, sleeve, and cap, his uniform was embroidered with an American flag with the wrong number of stars. His feet were bare. The sidewalk bustled with people, but many of them were not out-phased enough to notice the stranger. That was the most unnerving thing about the whole conmergence, Reggie thought, trying to decide if he should say something or just order his cappuccino. You could easily think you were schizo, or paranoid, seeing people fade in and out that no one else could see. Some people, even some scientists, still argued that the conmergence represented nothing more than mass hysteria, like the Salem witch trials.

He ordered and took a seat as far from the soldier as possible.

Mass hysteria or not, Reggie felt better when the crowd sipping their drinks at the tables outside Starbucks began to mutter and glance in the direction of the man with the gun. Others saw him; Reggie had not just imagined him, or at least, had not been alone in imagining him.

In a non-Euclidean universe, parallel lines can meet, and in a non-Euclidean multiverse, so can parallel universes. Scientists called it conmergence. Governments called it a threat. Some states had already passed laws to prevent illegal immigrants from other dimensions staying in-phase too long. As far as Reggie knew, no one could control it, no matter what the law books said.

The man with the gun had also noticed the crowd and the Starbucks for the first time. You could see it in his face. First, he paced some invisible beat with vicious boredom. Then he began to dart nervous glances this way and that way as he noticed flashes from the other phase. Finally, he found himself solidly in the middle of the noon-hour yuppie crowd, as out of place as a monster truck at an art museum. When the soldier realized where he was, his breathing quickened, and he gripped his gun.

Reggie didn't need the coffee. He was fully awake now.

The soldier threw the gun from him, suddenly. He raised his hands in the air.

"Plase," he said in strangely accented English. "Plase, don't hurt me. I surrender. Don't kill me. Don't send me back. Let me stay. I want to stay in this dimension. I demand asylum!"

His head jerked like a bird's, from one face to another. Reggie strategically sipped his cappuccino to avoid meeting the soldier's eyes.

The police arrived. Docilely, the soldier allowed them to take him away.

Comments on

"Conmergence"

Some writers are novelists by nature. Others excel at short stories. I'm definitely a 100,000 words-plus-size girl. I suck at short stories. And here you are reading my short stories... uhm, yeah. I meant to say, I find short stories "challenging." There, that sounds better. These stories don't suck, no sir. Would I make you read a collection of junk? Don't answer that.

Many of the stories in this anthology were originally novel ideas. Some, in fact, are extracts from novels. This one was only a wisp of an idea. I jotted down this scene and didn't know what else to do with it.

Then I discovered the magic of flash. Flash fiction: Really short stories that are often no more than that—a single flash of inspiration, a scene, a fragment. Wow, I guess I can write short after all! Somewhere deep in my heart, though, I still feel like I accidently left out 99,000 words.

THE PAINTED WORLD: PORTRAIT OF A PRETENDER

Part One: Waiting for Dusk

THE GASHES CROSSED HIS THROAT, chest, and thighs. Blood pooled like spilled paint beside him. His eyes bugged when Othmordian knelt and took his pulse.

"Why?" the dying man rasped. "Everything I gave.... Why wasn't it enough?"

The stateroom was furnished with fountains, mahogany chairs, rosewood tables, and gold-gilt pillars. On the walls, murals depicted scenery from each of the provinces of the Kingdom of Cammar. Each mural was tied off by a fat, velvet ribbon. Othmordian heard the sound of a boot scuffing the marble floor. There was someone else in the room, behind a jade-tiled fountain. Othmordian surged forward, his blood-wet blade still in his hand, and a young man deflected the attack with a kora, a hook-tipped sword. They circled, neither speaking, and steel clanged against steel. The young man fought like an animal, feral with rage, while Othmodian's style was precise and deadly. But just as he would have stepped in for the killing blow, a woman entered the room behind them.

She cried out, "Don't kill my son, Othy!"

The young man cut the velvet tie across a mural and leapt into the painting.

❏ ❏ ❏

The day after his brother's funeral, Othmordian could no longer put it off; he called an assembly to meet and name his new court. He took refuge in the formality of the occasion. In silence he let his brother's servitors swath him in belled garments of black and gold, in the tall heavy hat and the elaborate shoes, three pairs, one inside another, until his feet felt like clods of lead. They wrapped his injured hand in bands of silk. They anointed him in oils and lay a mint leaf on his tongue, while a tiny silver bell was rung four times four. With a swan's feather, they brushed white powder onto his brows and goatee, and they blackened the creases around his eyes with kohl, to make him look older and wiser than his three decades.

Othmordian hoped the illusion would help, but he doubted it. He had always been cleverer than Arnthom, but not more popular, and though people professed to love wisdom in a king, in truth they preferred charisma to intelligence.

Their preferences did not matter now. Arnthom was dead, and Othmordian must serve as regent until Arnthom's twenty year old son, Drajorian, reached his quarter century, when the fools assumed Othmordian would step down and glorious Drajorian, even more beloved than his father, would ascend the throne of Cammar.

Musicians plucked at nine-stringed instruments and moaned on three-throated flutes when Othmordian entered the Great Hall for the ceremony. In such ceremonies, one had to walk in just such a way: one foot dragging to meet the other, pauseing, the next foot extending slowly, setting down, pauseing, slow, slow, back ramrod straight, so carefully that not a bell on one's robe jingled. Othmordian made it to his place beside the empty throne of his dead brother without embarrassing himself too much.

The Four Officiants came forward to drone their hymns and chants. All went well until the Chant of Challenge, when the Officiants were required to ask of the Assembly whether anyone objected to the investiture of Othmordian as regent for his nephew.

The Officiants paused significantly in their chant, allowing ample time for all eyes in the room to turn to Prince Drajorian. Othmordian stiffened at their insolence, their unspoken accusation. He took care not to allow his frown to disturb his face.

The heir, Prince Drajorian, wore a veil under his tall moon-shaped hat, a veil to hide his face from hostile glamourers who might try to draw his portrait and thus capture his soul. The veiled prince stood ramrod straight and did not make any attempt to speak. Arnthom's closest allies, observing the heir's significant silence, guarded their own with sour frowns. Othmordian relaxed a fraction.

His relief was short-lived.

A woman stepped forward. In ringing tones, she announced, "I challenge."

You would, thought Othmordian.

Boldly, Lyadra met Othmodian's eyes. He nodded his head just a fraction, in wry acknowledgment. Princess Lyadra was Drajorian's betrothed. Once she had been Othmodian's betrothed.

"Princess Lyadra, your challenge is noted," the Four Officiants intoned. "In three days you shall present your case that the pretender is unfit or renounce your claim. Are there any others who would challenge?"

A susurration of unease rippled through the assembled notables.

Cowards, Othmordian cursed them in silent scorn. *There is not one of you here who does not suspect that I murdered my brother. Is only Lyadra brave enough to step forward to accuse me of what you all believe?*

After a thick, ugly, guilty silence, a second woman, twice the age of twenty-six year old Princess Lyadra rose.

"*I* challenge," she said.

Othmordian raised an eyebrow in surprise. His elder sister Forthia had been the one person he had *not* expected to accuse him. On the other hand, she and Arnthom had been closer in age and in sentiment than he had been with either of them.

"Princess Forthia, your challenge is noted," the Four Officiants sang. "In three days you shall present your case that the pretender is unfit or renounce your claim. Are there any others who would challenge?"

Othmordian felt his stomach clench. If a third challenged, and if all three refused to renounce their challenge in three days, he must face an actual trial for treason.

And naturally there was a third. Another woman—Drajorian's mother and Arnthom's widow, the Queen Mother Tulthana.

"I challenge," she said. Her white cape still smelled of funeral incense from her night spent in the company of her husband's corpse.

Three challengers. Schemes for dealing with Lyadra and Forthia already snaked through his mind. As for Tulthana—well, he would deal with her when the time came.

❑ ❑ ❑

Othmordian received Princess Lyadra in rich mahogany carved rooms lit with jasmine candles. Exquisite paintings in gilt frames vied for space on the walls. There were no portraits of men. Painting a living man would imprison his soul and was forbidden. Painting an imagined person was even more dangerous. Most of the paintings were of beautiful naked slave girls whose souls had been owned by past kings, or still lifes of food. Servants took a dozen still lifes from the walls and set them on the table, a painted feast of sausages, breads, cheeses and fruit. They tied ribbons around each painting, placed scissors next to the porcelain plates, then bowed and left.

Othmordian had chosen his wardrobe with care, a cape-coat of black and gold velvet over a buttercream silk blouse, similar to, but not quite as ornate as what he had worn before the Assembly. He'd washed his goatee and eyebrows of the white powder, so his hair was its natural ebony again. He smiled to himself when he saw that Lyadra wore a cream dress-coat and cloth-of-gold trousers, almost elaborate enough to be bridal. There was no doubt the warm whites and golds set her auburn hair and peaches-in-milk skin to advantage, but the presumption of her palette amused him. This woman had broken her betrothal to a poor artist in favor of his younger, but royally destined, nephew. She had not changed.

"Be seated, 'niece,'" Othmordian said mockingly.

"I will stand."

He shrugged. "I will sit."

From the canvases on the table, he chose a still life of a peach, plum and pomegranate. The scribbler, Habtheine, dead some centuries now, had been renowned for the rich pigments he had used to paint his plums and pomegranates, the translucent glazes he used to make his peaches glow. Othmordian cut the ribbons tied round the painting. The fruit tumbled onto his plate, round, juicy, solid. He sank his teeth into a peach. Sweet, sticky juice gushed in his mouth and dribbled from his lower lip.

"You dress like a prince now, but you still have the manners of a scribbler," Lyadra said with great distain.

"Ah, is that why you chose to forsake me in favor of my nephew, a boy six years your junior?" asked Othmordian. He dabbed his chin with a napkin. "His manners. I am sure that was especially evident when he was ten years old, which, as I recall, is when you made your decision."

Lyadra stared hard at him. "I always knew you were crass and unsocial, Othmordian. I never knew you were capable of murder."

"Why, I have no idea what you are talking about, Lyadra."

Lyadra smiled at him. "After a thought, I do feel a bit peckish. I think I shall accept your invitation to eat." She seated herself at the table and cut the ribbon on the painting of a glass of crushed lemon ice. She spooned a few bites onto her plate, which, however, she made no attempt to consume. "Beautiful food, by the way. Did you paint it yourself?"

"No, no. I'm afraid I haven't the talent to make my glamours real enough for a satisfying feast."

"That's odd," she said, "For I heard that in the years you lived at the glamourers' school, you developed quite a knack for magic. Perhaps even enough talent to draw a brink."

Othmordian smiled grimly. "Lyadra, do you even understand what a brink is?"

"Like a glamour, but it does not die at the twixting that divides day from night. Nothing can kill it. A monster painted and brought to life with blood from a human sacrifice. Such as the monster that killed your brother, Arnthom."

Othmordian took another bite of his peach. "This fruit feels solid, even tastes real. But when sunset falls, it will be as if I had never eaten it, for only the most skilled glamourers can paint the very essence of an object into their paintings. They must capture its very soul. If it is that difficult to paint the soul of a peach, imagine then how difficult it is to paint an imagined man with enough soul that he can escape the canvas and cross the twixting to breach the brink of our world. It's not enough to mix the paint with the blood of a human sacrifice. One must also have a master's skill." He finished eating and spit out the pit. "I assure you, I do not have that talent."

"I don't pretend to know about scribblings and glamours," Lyadra said with a dismissive wave of her hand. "But I know that King Arnthom was murdered. And I know that you've done something to Prince Drajorian. That veiled boy who walks around the palace like one of your soulless fruits—he is not human."

"You're right," said Othmordian.

Her jaw dropped, then her eyes narrowed.

"Your darling betrothed is actually a glamour," he said, "kept under careful control, redrawn each dawn and dusk, when the illusion fades to dust."

"I will bring this news to the Assembly..." Lyadra stood up.

"Will you?" Othmordian asked mildly.

Lyadra sat down again, horror on her pretty face. "Will you kill me and replace me with a glamour too, Othy?"

"Now I'm 'Othy' again," he noted. "You haven't called me that since you were sixteen."

"I never thought you capable of this," she said.

"No, if you had thought that I had a chance at the throne, you would not have cast me off in favor of my nephew."

"Is that why you murdered Drajorian?" she asked coolly. "To take revenge on *me*?"

How typical that she assumed everything revolved around her.

"Drajorian is not dead."

"Not...? Then where is he?"

Othmordian smiled. "Agree to renounce your challenge against me..."

...*And maybe I'll tell you,* was the unspoken implication, which, carefully, Othmordian did not actually promise aloud.

Lyadra stared at him wide-eyed for a moment. Then, as wax melted off a mold, her crafted veneer of affronted innocence melted away. The woman beneath the mask was harder, crueler. She burst into tinkling laughter. "Oh, Othy, Othy, Othy! Who knew you had it in you?"

Very deliberately, she picked up the plum from his plate and bit into it. She let the juice drip down her lower lip, and licked it off in a sensuous motion. "I'll go you one better. I will agree to marry you."

"Lyadra, I'm shocked."

"No. You are not. You knew that if you showed me the true extent of your power, I would flock to your side. Well. You were right. I presume that if the real Drajorian is not dead yet, he is your prisoner, and it is only a matter of time until you send him the way of his father."

"Would that bother you if it were true?"

"Not at all. But I want proof that he is your prisoner, that he did not escape you. Prove it to me by showing him to me—in chains. Then I will believe in your power and agree to be your queen." She grinned and leaned forward. "Oh, let me be the one to stick the dagger to the belly of the little brat."

Othmordian laughed. "In time, perhaps, Lyadra. But first you must prove yourself to me."

"I'll renounce my challenge." She shrugged.

"That's not enough."

"What else could you want?"

"Let me paint you."

She stood up, eyes flashing. "As if I were a slave girl? Are you mad?"

"I don't trust you. If I marry you, I must know I control you. You won't be humiliated. I'll keep the painting secret."

For a moment, he wondered if he had pushed too far, too fast. Her breath came rapidly and he watched, transfixed, how the translucent cream gauze of her blouse shimmered over her cleavage as her breasts rose and fell. How badly did she want to be queen?

"I will let you paint me," she said at last. "But there are two other challengers, Othmordian. And many, many others who suspect you. Your brother's death was messy. Even with no investigation by a master glamourer, everyone could tell he had been murdered by a brink. Very careless."

"Dear Lyadra, let me worry about that. Why don't you worry about the things you do best—your wardrobe on the day of your wedding—the day of *my* coronation."

"I want jewels," she said. "Silks and brocades. And a veyance pulled by the swiftest dogs. Every luxury must adorn my new station. If I'm going to sell my soul to you, I hope you do not think it will be cheap."

"You shall have all that you ask. Just be here at midnight to sit for your portrait."

She swept out of the room without answering. Although it was too soon for the glamour on the food to have worn off, his stomach clenched, as if empty. The table was full of food that would only leave him hungry. He tried to remember when he had last had a real meal, and realized it was before his brother had died.

❏ ❏ ❏

"I never liked that girl," Forthia said, stepping from the panel in the wall where she had been concealed. Her plum dress-coat was almost black. The tight leather pants she wore instead of the looser style more commonly favored by ladies made her look like a soldier. She had a kukri hooked on her belt.

Othmordian tried to not show that his older sister had taken him by surprise. He had not meant for her to overhear his sordid conversation with Lyadra. Also, it was nearly sunset. He did not have time for a long argument. Still, he had best not try to put this off.

"Forthia," he greeted her. "Did you spy on Arnthom as well?"

"You are not Arnthom," she said. "And to answer your question, yes, I often listened in on his privy councils from behind that panel, at his invitation."

"I don't recall inviting you."

"Perhaps you recall my challenging you," she said and pinned him with a look that made him feel eight years old again. "And after what I just heard..." She shook her head.

Othmordian sighed. He shoved himself back from the table. Glamoured food spoiled so quickly. The overripe scents only nauseated him now. He stood up and shrugged out of his black velvet cape-coat, then loosened the elaborate ruffles of the blouse at his neck.

"You had your reasons to doubt me before you overheard my sparring with Lyadra, else you would not have challenged in the first place. Well, pour out your accusations, then."

"It is a story of a moody child," said Forthia. "A stray child, his mother called him before she died, last born, when she thought her time for bearing past. Born the same year Arnthom married Tulthana, and during all the years they tried and failed to conceive a babe of their own, Arnthom would pat this stray on the head and promise him a throne. It was a blow to him when a real heir was born. Suddenly he went from heir apparent to being packed off to a lonely school on a distant moor."

"It was a relief to me, not a burden, to be spared the throne, Forthia," Othmordian said. "And as for the school, that was my request as well. I wanted to study magic. And I first went when I was thirteen, three years after Drajorian's birth."

"Yes," Forthia said, "I know. After you tried to kill him."

Othmordian frowned.

"No one told me," she said. "I have my ways of knowing."

"So I have discovered," he said dryly.

"If you were willing to kill your nephew when he was but a toddler, how much more so now that he the only remaining threat to your power?"

"And you think I killed our brother too?" Othmordian asked. His hand itched, and he toyed with the edges of the bandages, trying to scratch without removing them.

"There is more," she said.

"Say it then."

"No one allowed the glamourers to perform an investigation of our brother's death. Nonetheless, I secretly asked the Head Glamourer of Mangcansten Lodge to report his findings to me. He confirmed that Arnthom was killed by a brink. He also told me about your time as a student at his school, before you were expelled. And why you were expelled."

Vivid memories flashed across Othmodian's mind: the drunken smell of paint thinner, the sound of scribs on linen parchment, the giggles in the dark after the proctors extinguished the candles in the boys' dorm. Most wonderful of all, had been the early mist-filled mornings walking out alone on the moor, with only a sketchpad and a pack of wild dogs for company.

"He told me," continued Forthia, "That you were a mediocre artist, not a true glamour caster, except in one area. You could draw dogs like no one else, all kinds of dogs. He said that you even inquired into a forbidden area, how to make a certain kind of brink called a Smoke Hound. The Smoke Hound must be drawn with a burning coal. When it is brought to life, the hound moves with a hide of flame and smoke. The artist, however, is left with a burnt hand."

Forthia held out her palms. "Put your right hand in mine, Othmordian."

He did so. His right hand was swathed in bandages.

Tears pricked her eyes. "Oh, Othy." She released his hand. She drew a deep breath and looked him in the eye. "Have you anything to say to me?"

"Just this," Othmordian said. He caressed Forthia's cheek with his good left hand.

He glanced out the window, at the purpling western sky. He must soon attend to other matters. Time, time, he was running out of time. Fifteen minutes to sunset...five years to Drajorian's majority. He would not allow even Forthia to stop him.

"The Head of Mangcansten," she said in a low voice, "has promised me the support of his entire Glamourers' Lodge if I oppose you. As you know, all the notables who subscribe to Mangcansten will follow suit. You cannot hope to rule Cammar under such circumstances."

"Indeed, Forthia. But I have already communicated with the Head Glamourer of Langmar Lodge. They took me in after Mangcansten expelled me, and I have been their grateful supporter ever since. And vice versa. Langmar will uphold my claim to the throne, *even if* I am formally charged with treason by the Four Officiants of our late brother." He smiled without pleasure. "As you know, all the notables who subscribe to Langmar will follow suit."

The blood drained from her face.

"You are threatening civil war."

"No, big sister. *You* are threatening civil war. I am merely pointing out how closely matched the sides will be if you carry through your threat. It will divide the kingdom in half, Lodge against Lodge, noble against noble, sister against brother. Is that what you want?"

She did not answer, but for the first time, she looked her age, a decade and a half his senior. He knew that she would renounce her challenge on the third day for fear of destroying the whole of Cammar. Her shoulders slumped and she left bent over like an old woman.

□ □ □

As soon as Forthia had departed, Othmordian hurried from his chamber to the Northeastern Tower. A spiral staircase led him to the uppermost chamber, the Queen's secret atelier. She had once been a student at Langmar Lodge as he had, except that her skill, unlike his, would have been prodigious enough to make her a master glamourer, had she not been chosen as the wife of a king.

Queen Tulthana already sat at her easel, the veiled prince at her side, standing. A paint-splattered artist's apron covered her crimson dress-cape. She was close to fifty, yet remained a handsome woman. Now, however, she looked exhausted. Since her husband's gruesome death, her face had been etched with deep lines of pain and worry. She looked up as Othmordian entered the atelier.

"I feared you would not come," she said, "That you would seek to punish me for challenging you."

He did not answer at once. Instead he strolled to the far wall, which was covered with a large tapestry, embroidered with pomegranates, cypress trees and curling vines. He fingered a tasseled tie, but did not open the curtain.

"Why *did* you challenge me? I thought we had an agreement." He glanced at the veiled young man, the false Drajorian. "I wonder if you have decided to renege on our bargain."

"No, Othy." A pleading note entered her voice. "You hold the life of my son in your hands. After Lyadra and Forthia challenged you, I felt it would look strange if I did not as well. I also hoped to forestall any other challengers. If I took the position of third challenger, and then backed down, no trial could proceed."

"Ah."

"It would be Drajorian's death otherwise. I know that truth too well."

"I wondered if you had decided to try again."

"Never," she whispered.

"You should never have tried it in the first place." He stroked the bandages on his hand. It itched, but he couldn't scratch it. "It would have saved us all a lot of trouble if I had killed Drajorian when he was three."

"Please, Othy. Don't kill him."

"I only spared his life to please you, but you have to do your part, Tulthy," he said. "People are beginning to suspect I have the real Drajorian locked up in a dungeon. You have to give the new glamour a mouth."

"That would make it too easy to turn the glamour into a brink," she said. "If someone discovered what it was, and sacrificed a life to make it a monster...."

"Don't you trust me, Tulthy?"

He had to look away from the bleakness in her face. The tower had two large windows, one facing dawnward, one facing duskward. The eastern window was already showing stars, the western window glowed with dying ruby light. "It's time."

"Take off your veil," Tulthana instructed the silent young man.

The young man lifted the dark gauze. Where his face should have been was only a formless, parchment blankness. A moment later, the last sliver of sun dropped below the horizon. The blank faced man dissolved, leaving only a crumbled blank sheet of canvas paper and a ribbon where he had stood.

Othmordian let out a shuddering sigh. "Give the new one a face."

She nodded. She sketched a face onto her drawing, unclipped the parchment, and rolled it up in carefully knotted ribbons. She set it down on the floor. An instant later, a young man, veiled, twin in limb and stance to the one who had dissolved with sunset, stood there, silent and indifferent.

"Go to your bedroom, Drajorian," Tulthana instructed him. "Arise before dawn and come back here."

"Yes, mother," the glamour said in a hollow voice. Othmordian wondered how long that would fool anyone.

At dawn, this construct would dissolve, just as the other had. In the meantime, if anyone, servant or noble, checked in on "Prince Drajorian," he would appear to be right where he should be. No mystery unexplained. A lie covered by another lie.

The doppelganger drifted obediently from the room.

Othmordian tightened his jaw. He remembered watching Tulthy in the days shortly after Drajorian's unexpected birth had been announced. He remembered the pang he'd felt watching her cuddle the new baby, an empty feeling, like the hunger one felt after too much glamoured food. After his own mother had died, Tulthana had mothered him, and he had loved her so much that at night he used to lie awake, imagining how it would feel if she were killed too, just to brace himself against the pain. So he would be able to survive it.

He unsheathed the kukri he wore at his waist. He advanced toward Tulthana.

"And now, Tulthy," he said, "Now for the blood to bring the brink to life."

Part Two: Waiting for Dawn

He wiped the blood from his hands before he left the atelier.

He dined alone, on real food--plain, hard bread. The servants, as he'd instructed earlier, had a bath drawn for him when he reached his quarters. Steam rose like smoke from the big wooden tub and the water had been scented with mint. He scrubbed his bare skin until it reddened like boiled lobster. Dark, guilty thoughts made it impossible for him to relax. The memories were visceral: a metallic taste in his mouth, the sound of Tulthy's sobbing. He wished his dogs were here, but he had promised. He had made so many promises, hadn't he, and he was finding them harder than ever to keep. Dawn seemed far away.

The water cooled. The once clean water was now gritty with dead skin and it no longer felt good, but he did not leave the bath until he heard a soft knock on the door. Startled, he tossed on a robe.

Lyadra entered.

He stared at her.

"Midnight, you commanded me." She still wore lace and gold.

"Yes." He felt like an idiot. "I'm to paint you. Yes."

"Here? No servants answered my knock at the main door, so I just..."

"No, not here, in my studio. Come."

It was a typical studio, large, empty, with one bay window, which during the day provided excellent light. All it provided now was a backdrop of stars under a sliver moon. A pedestal, which usually held baskets of fruit, or other objects, such as knives, useful to glamour, stood in front of the window. He lit a dozen sconces one by one.

"No couch?" she asked. "No chains? Where do all the other slave girls pose for you?"

"You're the first."

"What honor you do me." Her voice was rich with sarcasm.

Without asking, she removed her clothes. Cream silk and gold brocade puddled at her feet. The shameless wench. No doubt she couldn't wait for the jewels he had promised her. She rested her hands on the pedestal. Auburn hair curled down her back, a cascade of corkscrews and curlicues. Her skin glowed like a Habtheine peach.

The first time he had seen her naked in the moonlight, she had smiled for him. They had both been so young, so in love—or so he'd thought. She did not smile now.

For a few moments, he studied her, saying nothing, nor moving. His fingers trembled when he reached for the jars of paint. Vermillion. Burnt Umber. Cadmium Red. Brushes, made from the fur of martens. Turpentine. The familiar scents, sharp and slightly alcoholic, reassured him. He set a new canvas on the easel and began to paint. He planned to paint wet on wet, with the sketch, underpainting and highlights all added swiftly, mixed on the canvas and done before dawn. He must finish before dawn.

The sketch went well. He outlined her pose, the angle of her head, the length of her calf. Firelight lit her from one side, starlight from the other. The mix of warm and cool struck him as evocative, the perfect way to capture her deceptive nature. But when he tried to draw her eyes, and the tiny frown lines around her lips, his strokes faltered. This was not working. He knew this painting could never capture her soul.

He put down his brush.

"Lyadra," he said. "Who has painted you before?"

Her lip quavered. "You can tell?"

"Did you give yourself to a lover? Body *and* soul?"

"It doesn't matter. It was a long time ago."

"You little idiot. If someone else has your soul, I cannot take it. His painting must be destroyed before mine can be finished."

She lowered her head and her hair veiled her face.

"Tell me his name," commanded Othmordian.

Still, she stayed silent. He smashed the canvas to the floor, rushed at her, and shook her. "Give me his name!"

He lifted her chin. Her hair fell away and he saw that her lips moved but no sound came out. She was weeping, but silently, help-lessly.

"The man who painted you, who bound your soul, he forbade you to reveal his name?"

She nodded. Even the slight motion seemed to cause her pain. After he released her, red smudges remained on her cheek, and for a heartbeat, he feared he'd somehow left blood stains, tainted her, but then he realized it was only paint, the dark mix of vermillion and burnt umber he had been using to capture the hue of her hair.

"When?"

He wasn't sure she'd be allowed by the geis to answer, but she replied, "Just before I broke my betrothal to you."

Years. She had been enslaved *years*. And he'd never guessed.

"You took a lover when we were still betrothed? You were just a girl."

"Believe what you wish."

"Are you able to tell me where he keeps the portrait of you?"

Again, it surprised him when she whispered, "Yes."

Yet why be surprised? What would her master have to fear? If he controlled her soul, he could command her not to touch the paint-ing, and she would have to obey, even if it were hanging on a wall in front of her. Those who had their souls stolen by painting could not destroy the art that enslaved them.

"Can you show me?"

"Yes." She knelt and clutched her cream and gold garments, twist-ing the cloth around her fingers. She glanced up at him. He had al-ways admired the translucent grey of her eyes, but now they looked opaque. "What will you do?"

"Destroy it."

"If you can't?"

"Is your lover a master glamourer?"

"May I dress?"

He nodded. Lyadra stepped into her pants, raised her arms and pulled on the lacey blouse. Her breasts jutted forward, and he had to resist the urge to pluck one like a peach and taste it. It infuriated him to think of another man, a real man, not a painted boy like Drajorian, touching her, tasting her, as Othy had when they had both been sixteen, in love with each other, themselves and the starlight. A moment later, she buttoned her jacket tight across her cleavage.

"I can have a dog carriage summoned," he said. He also dressed, and strapped on a kukri.

"No need. It's in the palace."

"You astound me. Lead on."

She walked without looking back. They traversed corridors lit only by infrequent pools of lamplight. The carpet gave way to stone and the cold seeped through his slippers. He wished he had taken the time to put on boots.

They reached a double door of thick, carved wood, which he did not recognize. He had seldom visited this part of the palace. She did not touch the bronze knobs, only waited. He pushed experimentally. Hinges creaked, the door swung inward. He entered first.

❑ ❑ ❑

Othmordian was not sure what he expected. A ceiling three stories high arched over a large hall, empty except for a cavernous fireplace at the far end. A fire blazed, two chairs before it. There were no other furnishings except thousands of paintings. Every space on the ample walls had been taken by a painting, large or small, until the walls looked like giant jigsaw puzzles.

Every picture was a portrait.

Most of the figures were shown head to toe: men in armor, holding kukris or pikes or crossbows. The largest paintings had dozens of figures, all martial. Each painting was tied with a dark plum colored ribbon.

The Painted Army. So it was real. He whistled.

"The one who enslaved me," Lyadra said bitterly. She pointed.

His sister Forthia rose from her high backed chair.

"Lyadra, step away," said Forthia. "You've done your part."

"This was a trap?" Othmordian asked Lyadra.

"I never had a choice," Lyadra. "Not when I broke my vow to you. Not tonight."

Forthia smiled sadly. "It had to be done, Othmordian. The royal family needed the alliance with Lyadra's lineage. Drajorian was the heir. But you were so besotted with her, and she with you, you refused to see that. I only did what I had to. Just as I do now."

She cut the ribbon on a large mural beside her. Twenty soldiers stepped out of the painting. Glamours, not brinks, but they would be invulnerable until dawn. They rushed him. He grabbed his kukri and split open the head of the first attacker, then spun and lopped off the arm of a second assailant. He slashed at a third, kicked a forth, but the odds were hopeless. Not only did the soldiers outnumber him, even those he downed would not stay down. The glamour whose head had split open slurped back together, and the armless man reattached his limb. The painted soldiers would always return to the way they had been painted, and they could not be killed. They surrounded him with bows and kukris drawn.

"I don't hate you, little brother," said Forthia. "I understand the jealousy that must have gnawed at you. First Drajorian took away Tulthy from you, then he took away Lyadra. Even if you didn't covet his throne, you would have hated him for that, I think. But you haven't killed him yet, and that was your mistake."

"I spit on your pity." He did spit. The glob of mucus struck the cheek of one of the soldiers, but the glamour did not blink, or wipe it away.

"And you were jealous, ultimately, because Drajorian was better than you. He was a decade your junior, but more of a man than you ever were. You were weak, sulky. All you wanted to do was daydream in a corner and draw dogs. He was a *man*. He is the perfect prince, handsome, strong, charming—all the things you are not, Othy. But if you will tell me where you are keeping the real Drajorian prisoner, I will spare your life."

"Ask Tulthy where the real Drajorian is," sneered Othmordian.

"I did not see her at dinner." Forthia's eyes widened. "No! You did not!"

The doors opened and the false prince Drajorian, the glamour, hurtled down the hall, howling. He attacked the soldiers surrounding Othmordian. It was glamour versus glamour. They hacked off his limbs but he regrew them; they smashed in his head, but it popped back out. They finally overwhelmed him with sheer numbers and bound him.

But Othmordian had not wasted the distraction. He lay about with his kukri, dismembering every glamour in his path to the fireplace. He reached his left hand into the hearth, and, ignoring the pain, squeezed a burning brand. A sketch: quick, sharp lines against the white inside wall of the fireplace, in the shape of a dog; followed by a palm print: blood from his blistered hand to bring it too life. The Smoke Hound jumped from the fireplace and tore into the glamour soldiers. They caught fire, the only thing glamours could not survive.

He strode to Forthia. She backed away until she was pressed against the wall.

"Am I weak now, Forthia?" he asked. "My scribbles have learned to bite."

"Are you going to kill me, Othy?" she whispered. "As you killed our brother and Tulthy?"

He reached his hand around her throat. She shut her eyes. He felt for the slim gold chain hidden beneath her jacket, and yanked it out hard enough to break the necklace. At the end of the necklace was a miniature of Lyadra, which he dropped on the flagstones and stomped. The shattered enamel cut through the sole of his slipper.

Behind him, he heard Lyadra gasp the moment the geis was broken.

"You should learn to look beyond the foreground, Forthia," Othmordian said. "Did it never occur to you to wonder if Drajorian was the perfect image of a prince because he was only that—an image? I cannot tell you where the *real* Drajorian is because I do not know. Because even the real Drajorian is not real." He raised his voice, "Isn't that right?"

A figure in a hooded, crimson cape-coat stood in the doorway at the other end of the hall. She stepped around the ashes of the battle. The Smoke Hound panted sparks at her, but did not stop her.

"I was young." Tulthana pushed back her dark red hood. "If I had only been content with you as an heir to begin with... It wasn't that I didn't love you, Othy. I just wanted a baby of my own so very, very much."

"I was glad to have a nephew," he said. "I had wanted to become a glamourer for some years, and it seemed an impossible dream. But—Tulthana—what you did—"

His eyes slid past her to the false Drajorian. There were no windows in the room, but the glamour prince and the Smoke Hound dissolved. A blank sheet of paper fluttered to the ground where the prince had stood.

"It's dawn, isn't it?" he asked. "We must make the blood sacrifice now."

"Yes," said Tulthana.

He released Forthia. He waved an invitation to her and Lyadra. "You are in this deep. If you are not afraid of the truth, come with us."

"No," said Tulthana.

"You cannot keep this from Forthia any longer," he said, "And I will not keep it from Lyadra."

Tulthana bowed her head. "Then come," she said. "See my folly, for which I have paid dearly."

❑ ❑ ❑

On the third day, Othmordian stood once more on the dais before the assembled notables and four Officiants. Today, all would learn whether he would next be charged for regicide and high treason or anointed Regent and married to his nephew's former betrothed. The three women who had stood to challenge him three days before, stood now in a row before him, youngest to eldest.

The First of the Four Officiants stepped forward.

"Challenger the First, Lady Lyadra," intoned the old man. "Do you stand fast to your challenge or do you renounce it?"

Lyadra met Othmodian's eyes. For a moment, he allowed himself to admire the sheen of her auburn hair falling over a peach gown. Each bell-accented curve of her body tinkled as she moved. She was beautiful, he thought, with a twinge of his old heartache.

"I renounce my challenge," she said smoothly. The audience of notables shifted uneasily at her response. Othmordian allowed some of his grim satisfaction to show. The rabble had wanted blood. Too bad.

Even the supposedly neutral First Officient frowned. However, he continued the formal ceremony without demure.

"Challenger the Second, Princess Forthia," he said. "Do you stand fast to your challenge or do you renounce it?"

Forthia stood tall in royal purple. "I renounce my challenge."

The First Officient glanced sidelong at Othmordian. By now the old man must have known how the rest would go, although from the old man's angry frown, he'd no idea how Othmordian had convinced all three challengers to back down.

"Challenger the Third, Queen Tulthana," said the First Officiant. "Do you stand fast to your challenge or do you renounce it?"

"I renounce it," said Queen Tulthana.

A vast, almost soundless, yet palpable groan passed through the hall. So. The Pretender was judged no pretender, but the legitimate Voice of the Throne. No one who still suspected Othmordian of murdering his older brother would dare make that accusation openly now.

The Four Officiants began to chant, resuming the ceremony of investiture as Regent that had been interrupted by challengers three days ago. Othmordian hardly heard them.

"Prince Othmordian," the First Officient addressed him. "Will you accept the responsibility of Regent until such time as your nephew, Crown Prince Drajorian, comes of age and ascends the throne as King of Cammar?"

After Forthia had learned the truth, she had agreed with him, that, if necessary, he must kill Drajorian. But if Tulthana's hope proved right and there was a chance that this entire pretense could be made real? If it required that Othmordian bleed himself, body and spirit, every day for another five years, it would be worth the price.

"I will," said Othmordian.

❏ ❏ ❏

Another dusk. Another visit to Tulthana's atelier. The difference was that Lyadra accompanied him up the steps of the tower.

"You don't have to come with me every time," he said. "Only Tulthy and I have to be there each dusk and dawn."

"I wished to speak to you," she said. "About our...marriage. When you first proposed it, after my challenge, I only agreed because I thought you would murder Drajorian if I did not."

"I understand." He sighed. "I release you from that promise. And of course, I will destroy the painting I began of you. I did wrong to start it."

"I knew you thought I only wanted the wealth and power of the position. Because I thought you were...you had...well, I didn't care what you thought of me. But I care now. I don't...even if we can save Drajorian, I cannot marry him."

"Of course not. Not now that you know."

"That's not what I mean. I am in love with someone else. If he would still have me."

They came to the top of the stair.

"You would marry me even if I never became king?" Othmordian asked.

"Do you still think I ever cared about that?"

No one could see them. He kissed her. "This will only convince everyone I am after the throne, you know. They'll be sure I want your father's gold."

"Do you care what they think?"

He laughed, ruefully. They entered the atelier.

Tulthana waited by the pomegranate curtain, and she pulled it open to reveal large, life-size oil painting with a scenic landscape in the background, and, in the foreground, a blank silhouette the shape of a missing man.

Othmordian wondered what would have happened if his first attack on his nephew had succeeded. Back then, Othy had been a boy of thirteen, and Drajorian had been three. This same canvas, in those days, had shown a toddler. At first, upon finding the painting, Othmordian had thought that someone had captured Drajorian's soul. Only the lack of ribbons tied around the painting had revealed the truth, that Drajorian was a brink. Even so, Othmordian had not guessed the whole of the matter, but assumed that some evil glamourer had tried to draw a monster to take the flesh-and-blood Drajorian's place. How could he have guessed that his beloved aunt and uncle had used magic to create the baby they could never have naturally?

"Thank you for doing this, Othy," said Tulthana, "It was not Drajorian's fault that I brought him into this world. He could not help what he was. He could not help that he had no soul."

Or that, like the monster he was, Drajorian killed his own father, then fled the palace before Othmordian could stop him. But Othmordian did not say it aloud. It had all been said. Most brinks were given the power to cross the twixting by a human sacrifice. Tulthana and Arnthom had been convinced there was another way. They had not killed anyone to mix the paints for his portrait. They drew their own blood, day after day, a little at a time, in the belief that if both a man and woman give one drop of blood each day for twenty-five years to a brink, they could imbue him with a soul. Unfortunately, until then, he was still a brink: picture perfect prince on the outside, soulless monster on the inside.

Five more years of blood, every sunrise, every sunset, from a man and a woman, was needed to give Drajorian a soul.

"Do you really think I can take Arnthom's place?" Othmordian asked. "If my brother's daily blood was not enough to give soul to the brink, how then a pale substitute?"

"You promised to try."

"I know, Tulthana, I know." Secretly, however, he felt a heavy weight inside. He did not think Drajorian would ever grow a soul no matter how much blood Tulthana or anyone else poured out.

Lyadra touched his arm. Though she said nothing, her trust glowed in her face.

Othmordian tightened his jaw. He unsheathed his kukri. Then he unwrapped his bandaged right hand, exposing the scars from the previous cuts to his palm. He dug the dagger into his flesh again. Tulthana did the same. Drops like pomegranate seeds fell into an empty paint jar. Lastly, she picked up a paintbrush, and as she had every day for twenty years, began to mix the tiny drops of blood into the still wet oils of the painting.

Comments on

"Portrait of a Pretender"

I started this story to revisit an old trope: the murdered king, the scheming uncle with pretensions to the throne, the endangered heir. I wanted to give the scheming uncle's perspective. The title and Prince Drajorian's name are a hat tip to The Portrait of Dorian Gray, and the theme of surface versus soul.

This is another chapter that wandered away from a novel and fell into a short story. You'll find another installment in this anthology, *Drawn to the Brink*.

REFRACTIONS FROM THE NEGLECTED SIDE

A FINGER WIGGLED in front of my nose.

"What do you see?" asked Dr. Chopra.

"Your finger moving."

"Fine, good," said Dr. Chopra. "Keep your eyes fixed on the same spot, the tip of my nose, just like before. Now what do you see?"

I waited but noticed nothing in particular, so I said nothing.

"Ms. Link?" the doctor prompted.

"I'm ready whenever you are, Doctor," I said, a touch impatiently.

"Ms. Link, don't you see my finger wiggling, just the same as before except that now it is to your left rather than your right?"

Surprised, I looked again, and saw Dr. Chopra's vivacious digit dancing at the end of his hand.

"Oh, yes," I said sheepishly. "But surely you weren't doing that before?"

"Oh, I was, you just didn't notice it," Dr. Chopra said amicably. "Now, I want you to look at these two pictures."

He took out two flash cards, each with a drawing of a house. He stacked them one on top of the other. The pictures were identical.

"Tell me what differences you see between the two pictures," he suggested.

"Ah, well, I was never much for 'Where is Waldo' games," I muttered. I searched the two pictures for absurd little inconsistencies such as upside down porch lights or fish in the bird's nest in the tree. I finally gave up.

"Well, but surely there is one you would prefer to live in," suggested Dr. Chopra.

"But, Doctor, it's the same house!"

"Humor me. If you *had* to choose, which would you rather move into?"

There was something about the bottom house that I didn't quite trust, although I couldn't say why. With a shrug, I said, "The top house."

"Why?"

"No reason, Doctor. I just prefer it."

"Not because the left side of the bottom house is depicted as being on fire?"

"What? You're kidding. What are you talking about?"

"I assure you, it's right there in the picture. You failed to notice the left side of the pictures."

"Am I going blind, Doctor?" I asked anxiously. "I don't seem to have any trouble seeing, but strange things keep happening. My husband says that I only eat half of what's on my plate unless he rotates it halfway around during dinner. People at work have told me that I've come in with my make-up and hair only half done, the other half completely unkempt. But I could swear that in the mirror each morning I curled my hair and put on my lipstick and mascara just as usual. People claim that they have been standing next to me, trying to get my attention and I acted like I didn't see them. I don't understand it."

"You're not going blind. You simply have a condition known as hemineglect. To state it simply, your brain no longer 'notices' the entire left side of your world. It says here in your case history that you were in an automobile accident and sustained a head injury? To the right hemisphere?"

"Yes, the right hemisphere," I admitted. I knew that the left hemisphere controlled the right side of the body and the right hemisphere controlled the left side of the body, so I asked, "Doctor, is that why I have lost the ability to notice 'left'? If I had damaged the left side of my brain, would I have lost the ability to notice 'right'?"

"Probably not, Ms. Link," he said. "When it comes to the elusive job of 'paying attention' the symmetry of our brain is not perfect. The left side of the brain is already preoccupied with language, so it has fewer resources to devote to attention. It covers paying attention to right side of your world, as would be expected. The right side of the brain, in contrast, is the more holistic of the two; it somehow has the ability to focus on both left and right. So, if you had suffered damage to your left hemisphere, you probably would have continued to notice both sides of your world. On the other hand," he spread his hands apologetically, "You might not have been able to talk about it."

"Is there any cure?"

"There are no guarantees, but there are options. One is the stimulation of renewed cell growth in the affected area. But that is experimental, only a last resort if you chose to try it. First, I'd like to try some non-invasive procedures that may help in retraining your brain to see 'left' with out extreme measures."

❑ ❑ ❑

At my next appointment, Dr. Chopra asked me to sit in a chair in front of a table. He put a pen on the table behind my right shoulder, then stood in front of me with the mirror.

"What am I holding, Ms. Link?"

"What do you mean, what are you holding? A mirror."

"Do you know how a mirror works?"

"I may be brain-damaged, Doctor, but I'm not stupid."

He smiled. "Do you see the pen? Would you please pick it up?"

I could see the pen on the table behind me, reflected in the mirror in front of me. With no trouble, I reached over my shoulder and picked it up.

"Very good, Ms. Link," he said.

Dr. Chopra moved the table away to somewhere else. Then he stood by my right side, again holding the mirror.

"Do you see the pen?"

I saw the pen reflected in the mirror. But the odd thing was that it wasn't reflected from anywhere, which meant that it must actually be behind or within the mirror somehow. I put my hands to the mirror, trying to reach through it, then around it and behind it.

"Don't grab the reflection, grab the pen itself," Dr. Chopra urged.

"I'm trying," I said, "But the mirror is in the way."

"Ms. Link, the pen is on your left side, the reflection is on your right side. Just like before, when the pen was behind you and the mirror in front of you, remember?"

Unfortunately, this case was completely different, because the pen reflected out of nowhere. Perhaps, I thought, the light is bouncing off it very strangely, like colors through a prism. But I couldn't backtrack properly how that would position the pen, except to try reaching under and then over the mirror. Neither tactic worked.

Finally, Dr. Chopra sighed. He put down the mirror and picked up the pen out of nowhere – perhaps he had had it the whole time.

"For some patients with hemineglect, mirror work can enable them to perceive the left side, and gradually retrain their brains to do so regularly. In certain other cases, the damage has apparently been more comprehensive. This appears to be your case. There are still other tests I would like to perform, but perhaps you might begin to consider if you want to go the other route."

❑ ❑ ❑

After another six frustrating months of having to take turns sitting on opposite sides of the breakfast table for fifteen minutes each in order to eat my whole plate, I was ready for the experimental cell growth stimulation procedure. It proceeded slowly, with the doctors, including Dr. Chopra, monitoring my progress carefully. All seemed to go quite well, knock on wood. According to Dr. Chopra, by the end of the series of treatments, I now had more active synapses in the part of the right hemisphere devoted to attention than I had ever had in my life. The doctors expected most of the additional neural connections to die back, leaving me with a normal number.

❏ ❏ ❏

I laughed when I saw the pictures I had drawn for Dr. Chopra when I had been suffering from hemineglect: flowers with the petals all to one side, houses with windows and roof on only one side, one sided clocks and lopsided number lines! My drawings for Dr. Chopra were now quite normal. I also passed the wiggling finger test with flying colors.

As for the headaches, Dr. Chopra didn't like the sound of that, but he assured me it was probably nothing to worry about as long as they did not persist. He did urge me to mention if I noticed anything else amiss – or if any of my nearest and dearest noticed anything I missed.

I felt I was doing better, and my friends and family agreed. In fact, I appeared to finally have a run of good luck. I work in a tall building, with a four-elevator lobby. It's always a guessing game which elevator will arrive first, but I found that now my guesses were invariably correct. I found it easier to find parking spaces. I no longer lost my way on strange roads.

❏ ❏ ❏

"Doctor, now I'm seeing things," I complained to Dr. Chopra.

"What kinds of things?"

"It's hard to explain. I see things before they happen. Not very far in advance, only a few seconds or a minute at most. Especially in mirrors. It's as though I catch a glimpse of something that isn't reflected from anywhere, just like when you gave me that pen test. But then it always arrives a second or two later, just as I saw it in the reflection."

"Well." Dr. Chopra considered this. "Would you like to try the mirror test again?"

"Yes."

He set it up, just as before, first placing a pen behind me while he held the mirror in front, then to each side of me. I had no trouble, on this occasion, reaching for the pen opposite each reflection.

Then something strange happened.

Quite clearly, I saw Dr. Chopra's assistant walking down the hall and open the door to his office. The angle was quite odd, as if it were only a reflection *but I did not see it in the mirror.*

"Your assistant is coming," I said to Dr. Chopra.

"What makes you think so?"

"I saw her reflection."

"Dr. Chopra, here is the Minsky file—" said the secretary, opening the door to his office and setting a file on the table.

"I knew it," I said. "I saw her."

"You must have heard her coming," Dr. Chopra said.

I might have believed him if this had been the first time it had happened.

❏ ❏ ❏

Dr. Chopra and the other doctors on my case were quite disappointed with me because my perception problems worsened. I began to see "doubles" of people, as if they were both near and far from me at the same time. I couldn't tell if an object was on my right or on my left – sometimes it appeared to be both. I almost lost my license after I crashed my car into a semi. I hadn't been able to tell if the intersection had been in front of me or behind me, if the light had turned green yet or remained red. I became confused about the sequences of things, sometimes seeing things reflected before they happened, other times seeing events repeated after they happened.

Convinced that the procedure had been a failure and that my brain damage crippled me more than ever, I stopped going out much beyond my daily commute to and from work. I took the train rather than drive. I wondered how long I could continue to function to even this conscribed degree. There were times that the train appeared to be coming in two opposite directions at once.

By now my world had turned into a kaleidoscope. I saw doubles and triples and multiple reflections everywhere. Some showed the future, some the past, some a simultaneous instant but from a wholly odd angle. My overactive perception had turned the once rational universe into a funhouse mirror maze.

Brain scans revealed that the neural growth stimulated by the procedure had died back, just as the doctors had predicted. But for me, ironically, this pruning of neurons had been accompanied by an exaggeration of the quixotic flaws in my perception, not a reduction. In an attempt to cheer me up, Dr. Chopra joked that if before I had suffered hemineglect, I now suffered from hemihyperactivity. I chuckled only weakly because he also admitted he had no idea how to help me.

❑ ❑ ❑

I avoided family and friends and spent most of my time holed up in the den, surfing the net. Consciously, I had given up on searching for medical answers to my condition, but unconsciously, I guess I still wanted a philosophical explanation for it.

I found the answer in the last place I expected--a university website on astrophysics.

Astrophysicists, it seems, are concerned about the possibility that our universe might be infinite. For a variety of reasons, some argue that it must be finite. The problem is that measurements of the rate of expansion since the Big Bang indicate that our universe is hyperbolic, or in other words, that spacetime is negatively curved.

The reconciliation between these two arcane pieces of evidence could be that our universe has a "nontrivial" topology. Instead of being a simple plane or sphere, in other words, our universe could possess a rather complex shape.

For instance, suppose our universe were a cube in which the right side of one cube corresponds to the left face. This would result in video game rules of movement: exiting the right side of the screen would cause you re-enter on the left side. If you stood directly in the center of the cube and looked either to the left or right, you would see an apparently infinite number of reflections of yourself, turning your head in synchrony with you. If you stood a little to one side of the cube, the light from the closer face might hit you faster than the light from the far face, allowing you to see into the "future" and see yourself turn your head in the reflection you appear to do so, while the light lagging from the far side would show a delayed reflection of your past. In fact, of course, all activities would be simultaneous, and you couldn't change the future.

Our 3-dimensions of space are almost certainly embedded in a larger number of hyperdimesions, but the theorists don't agree how many or what transdimensional shape our universe ultimately takes. Scientists search astronomical data for evidence of "ghosts" or reflections of the same galaxies repeated over and over in the night sky. Such reflections would indicate that we dwell in a nontrivial space.

What if the search did not have to be so far afield? What if we lived our lives literally surrounded by refractions from the hypershape of our universe, but were blind to it?

We assume, naively, that our senses evolved to reveal to us the construction of reality. Not a bit of it. Our senses evolved to provide us with the information we needed to stay alive. What our brains allow us to perceive is controlled by what input our brains evolved to process. As I had discovered for myself, once my brain decided that the left side of the universe no longer needed to exist for me, it effectively ceased to exist as far I was concerned. If every other human being had lost the ability to perceive left sidedness at the same time as I had, not one of us would have ever known there was anything wrong with us.

What if there was *another* side, neither right nor left, up nor down, that our brains had never evolved to perceive? If that were true, then even if information, such as light refraction, reached us from that other side, *we would simply ignore it*. If we all ignored it together, there would be no one to point out our mistake to us.

I started leaving the house again. I had an idea. I began to exercise my new sense of perception, experiment with it. I became more and more convinced that my hunch was right. There existed not just *one* "other" side, but *many*. Depending on where I stand in relation to the "faces" of the hyper-shape in which we live (it isn't as simple as a cube, but I haven't figured out exactly what it is yet) I can catch reflections of a few seconds into the future or see replays of a few seconds from the past. I can see people I am speaking with from the front and back at the same time. I can watch my own reflection from around corners. I knew the correct answers to questions by peeking into my own future and noting what I replied. Once I saved myself from a mugging by spotting myself in the future avoid walking by a dangerous spot. (There was no time paradox because I saw myself do what I did.) My newfound talent also proved useful for finding parking spaces.

All these doubles and reflections and time asynchronies used to bewilder and frighten me, but now that I've learned to intuit the topological rules of the game, I can use it to my advantage. So, the last question is, if what I perceive now represents both a more accurate picture of the shape of reality and it gives me a personal advantage in dealing with others, why can't everyone do it? Why did our brains evolve to teach us to *ignore* rather than *perceive* such an important aspect of reality?

I suspect I know the answer. The perceptive faculties of our brains are basically not much different than those of cows, lizards, and fish. Yes, in general, perception has increased along with brain size and complexity. The vertebrates have more complex senses than the invertebrates, the higher mammals may see in more detail and color than the lower mammals. But the trend doesn't always hold. Dogs smell better than we do, and bats echolocate better than either of us. Nature can discard extraneous senses as well as refine them.

Most animals can't recognize themselves in a mirror. If they notice their reflection at all, they assume it is another animal and try to flee or attack it. Perhaps the same thing happens to animals that perceive the extra sides of reality. I myself found it very confusing, especially the time distortions. It wasn't until I studied the theory behind the topology of higher dimensions that I comprehended what I perceived well enough to exploit it.

Until the existence of the human neocortex, capable of complex imagination, planning and memory, no animal brain existed for whom it *would* be an evolutionary advantage to perceive the extra sides. Previous animals didn't need to see from those angles, so they ignored them.

But then, how had stimulating growth in my brain enabled *me* to see them? A seed of the ability must have already been planted in the structure of my brain.

Something Dr. Chopra had said niggled at me. When the left hemisphere suffered damage, the victim did not experience a loss of the sense of the right side. Somehow the right hemisphere compensated and allowed the person to retain a sense of both left and right.

What if there was a latent ability of the right hemisphere to see some of the other dimensions? The brain normally repressed or subordinated the ability as a mere reinforcement of the normal perceptions of left and right and up and down. Yet it existed, and even ordinary people might have a glimpse of it at times when flashes of insight came to them about the immediate future or an event just out of their ordinary perception. "Extrasensory perception" would be a misnomer. The senses involved, mostly sight (for humans), were quite mundane. Only our ability to *notice* what we sensed changed. The talent should be called "extraperceptory sensing."

Evolution never stops winnowing new tricks. If the capacity to imagine and comprehend topology made the ability to perceive nontrivial topology an advantage for me, it must be an advantage for other *homo sapiens* as well. All of us had already evolved a right hemisphere able to dimly perceive the other sides. Just by the luck of the genetic draw, the talent would be greater in some than in others.

Somewhere in the world today, there must be people who have the same talent I do, not because of a medical procedure but because of a natural genetic quirk that meant they were born with a larger part of their brain devoted to perception of the hyperspace dimension. I want to find them. If they really are the next wave of hominid evolution, then one day in the future there will probably be a conflict between the hyperhominids and *Homo sapiens sapiens*. When that day comes, I want to be on the right side.

Comments on

"Refractions From The Neglected Side"

If I had a second brain, and if that brain could pass Calculus (un-like my first brain) I would use it to be a neurologist. Have you no-ticed how many neurologists are also brilliant storytellers? Or per-haps it is just that Oliver Sacks opened the field of neurological case studies as a genre. Either way, I am thankful.

Hemineglect or hemi-inattention, is a real condition. It is men-tioned in the case of Mrs. S, in "Eyes Right!" of *The Man Who Mis-took His Wife for a Hat*, by Oliver Sacks. My scientist, Dr. Chopra, is loosely inspired by V.S. Ramachandran, who wrote about another case of hemineglect in his book *A Brief Tour of Human Conscious-ness*. Ramachandran designed the mirror tests described in the story. Incidentally, Ramachandran also predicted the existence of mirror neurons, which have been discovered to be of importance in how we empathize with other human beings, how we learn, and how we imagine other minds. Without mirror neurons, there could be no novelists.

In this story, I tried to imagine what hemineglect would feel like to the person suffering it. And then I tried to take that one step further.

BURN
(8 OF SWORDS)

IN THAT KINGDOM, witches burned. Sir Grethory, a Templar of the Omniscient, one of the Eight, was sent to capture the witch known as Elieth. His blessed sword led him to where she hid in a barn. Her tendrils of soot dark hair smoked around her pale shoulders, and her eyes, two coals, smoldered in her fr ightened face. His gauntleted hand curled around her wrist as if around the neck of a tiny, trembling, woodland creature. Madness moved him, or magic, or love.

"Marry me," he whispered to her, "And I will safeguard you."

Fear forced her, or despair, or love, to say yes. He took her to his manor, where he married her according to the sacrament of the Omniscient. Each night, he cut her eight times to hide her essence from the other seven Templars who hunted witches with their swords blessed by the Temple. One stroke cut away her beauty, which had the look of a witch. The second cut away her laugh, which had the sound of a witch. Three, four, five and six cut away the fragrance of her skin, the touch of her hand, the taste of her and those of her movements that were the movements of a witch. Seven pared down her words. Eight cut away those of her thoughts that were the thoughts of a witch.

The blessed sword that found thoughts was Sir Grethory's own, and by it he had found her that first night. By the beauty of her thoughts as much as of her flesh, he had loved her. Yet now he cut down her thoughts, to better safeguard her. Such was his love, or his magic, or his madness.

Thus dragged years. Each night, he cut her and caged her. Each morn, Elieth awoke paler, weaker, less herself. When they went out to a fete at the Temple or at the castle of the king, she lifted no bite of food to her mouth save first she checked whether his brows knotted or lifted to chide her for gluttony or encourage her to eat more. In Grethory's home -- she belonged to it more than it belonged to her -- she strained her ear for the weight of his footfall and the tenor of his sigh, to judge whether his mood demanded her in his bed or away from it. A sunny day in the garden would be eclipsed by his frown; a romantic dinner by moonlight would be an ordeal to nurse his smile.

The morning came when Elieth awoke too weak to rise from bed. She wilted towards dying.

Vaguely, she knew when Grethory loomed over her bed. Seven others stood with him.

"A pity," one of the other Templars murmured, clapping Grethory on the shoulder.

"Yes," Grethory said. "It will be hard to find another witch with as much magic in her eight essences for me to siphon into my sword. Yet how rewarding the irony that all these years the demon's blood has sustained the work of the Omniscient."

Then at last did Elieth understand how the Templars quarried their prey, not with a single stroke, but with a thousand.

"Up, witch," said Grethory. He slapped her face.

The Eight Templars lifted her from the bed, bound her hands behind her back, and marched her to gibbet before the Temple. There they surrounded her with their blessed swords, preparing to perform the sacrament of holy murder.

Elieth had not been weakened so much as they supposed. She reached into her eight essences. She combusted. The blaze that exploded around her tossed aside the cage of swords. The Eight Templars caught fire. Their roasting flesh and burning robes smelled like pork and saffron. They fell to the ground, screaming, trying to roll out the flames. Still ablaze, Elieth strode away from that Temple, free for the first time.

In that kingdom, witches burned.

Comments on

"Burn (8 of Swords)"

I have an ongoing project to write a story for every Tarot card in the deck. Two are included in this anthology. Ideally, I try to work in the motif of the card—in this case, eight swords—into the story in a way that makes sense. The most important thing, however, is to try to capture the spirit of the card. Eight of swords traditionally shows a woman chained up, and represents a block, a stoppage, detention, jail, or prison. For writers, it can signify writer's block. One day, I hope to illustrate each story and create my own deck.

This particular tale was inspired by a bad break up. (Surprise, surprise!) I worked so hard to please someone else that I found I was strangling myself for his sake. I did not explode literally, but I did burn a calendar, in the presence of some good friends, to formally rid myself of the year I had spent wasting my love on someone who returned only recriminations.

This story is also a tribute to the thousands of women murdered as witches during "the Burning Times." Actually, thousands of people are still harassed and even murdered every year because they are accused of being witches. It's rather awful.

I studied Tarot for many years. I do readings for friends and family, and have even done readings professionally. Despite my love of Tarot, and my ability to do Tarot readings, I don't "believe" in Tarot cards. That is, I don't believe they can tell us anything we didn't already know. Sometimes, however, we know things we don't want to admit we know, or that we prefer not to think about. In those cases, Tarot is useful to jog our thoughts. Meditating over the images can free new associations in our minds, allowing us to see old things in a new light.

THE BEST OF ALL POSSIBLE WORLDS

PERSONAL PARADISE INC. did not buy ads in the *Chicago Tribune* or post notices on the Internet. They relied strictly on word-of-mouth. Their clientele were ubiquitously as discrete as they were rich.

The office of Personal Paradise Inc. reflected the nature of the company: quietly opulent. Exquisite and unidentifiable masterpieces of famous artists graced the walls, boasting silently: *We were made in another history.* Glass shelves framed Declarations of Independence to start nations that had never existed, and Treaties of Perpetual Peace to end wars that had never been fought. Photographs showed cities where all the cars had three wheels and the pedestrians wore fashions subtly wrong. Despite himself, Dean was impressed.

Klaas Smit was a white-haired man with a florid face and immaculate suit. His office was dominated by a large photographic mural of Manhattan: a Manhattan with a skyline not quite right, a nude Statue of Liberty, Dutch flags.

"So," Dean said without preamble, as he seated himself across from Smit. "Have you found me a world where I am richer and more powerful than I am in this dump?"

"We have found the best of all possible worlds for you." Smit leaned forward over steepled hands. "You'll be happiest man on Earth."

Dean reflected on his life: his company, once his baby, now his slave driver; his parents, to whom he had not spoken in years; Colette, grown more and more distant. None of it made him happy.

Smit displayed a map of the alternate Earth that the company had identified as Dean Vanch's personal paradise. The map of the other Earth looked like a three-day binge of Risk. Outlandish politics resulted in familiar landmasses with unfamiliar borders.

"France won the French-Indian wars," Klaas Smit said affably. "Among others. But don't worry—by the early Twenty-first Century, Napoleon's empire has long since collapsed in on itself. It will be nothing but history for you. Here is where your alternate self lives."

Smit pointed to a nation gathered around the Great Lakes, between New England and Louisiana, labeled "Acadia." The capital city read: DIESKAU, although it was located where Detroit should have been.

Smit cheerily outlined the history of Acadia. Like most of the nations in North America, it had achieved independence in the 1830s, trading an imperial dictatorship from abroad for a home-grown "presidential" dictatorship. Because of ethnic tensions, Acadia's fitful bouts of democracy had been pockmarked ever since with military coups and civil wars. Acadia had, in some ways, fared better than other North American nations. Take French Mexico, with 159 coups in 170 years since independence, or California, which, after thirty years of fascist rule followed by forty years of Communism, had no economy or industrial infrastructure worth mentioning.

In recent years, Acadia, like many of its neighbors, had been engaged in bouts of vicious ethnic cleansing, as the Anglophones and Francophones took advantage of their turns in power to exterminate one another. The country funded its forty-years-and-going civil war with a brisk cocaine trade.

To Dean, it sounded like Eastern Europe's 20th Century piled on top of South America's 19th. "*This* is the best of all possible worlds? Weren't there any with nuclear winters available?"

Smit smiled slyly. "Remember! What matters isn't if the world makes *most* people happy, only if it makes *you* happy!"

Dean had a sudden vision of himself as supreme dictator of one of these states, with palaces, cars, women, and the power of life and death over his subjects. He grinned.

"Damn straight. As long as I'm happy, screw the rest. Let's do it."

❑ ❑ ❑

He felt nothing during the transfer itself, but immediately a cold, gritty wind began to blast him. He found himself next to naked and the temperature next to freezing. He gawked at his surroundings. Barbed wire. Thin, half dressed men. Sky blown with ash and smoke. For some reason he was holding a heavy rock. What the *hell*...?

Dean stepped out of line with the shuffling men. They, too, carried large rocks. He dropped his to the ground.

Pain snapped across his back. He cried out and crumbled to the ground, full of surprise and then indignation.

"Work, you lazy dog!" a voice growled.

Dean almost laughed. The absurdity overwhelmed him. A thug in an unrecognized uniform had hit him with a *whip*. Then anger replaced irony. He recognized a damn labor camp when he saw one. And it was clear he wasn't running it. Personal Paradise Inc. had betrayed him.

Dean would have tackled the guard. Except Dean's body had changed too. His attempted tackle degenerated into a wheezing struggle just to regain his feet. Dizziness, nausea and aching limbs made movement itself an agony. His body, which had been sleek with gym-worked muscles before the transfer, was putty stretched across bone. That dull pain in his distended stomach—that was hunger. Starvation. Real starvation, not the damn-it-why-don't-you-have-anything-decent-prepared-I'm-starving starvation he had often bitched about at Colette.

The whip descended again. Dean Vanch cringed, and felt shame at cringing, but it *hurt*.

"If you're too weak to work..." The guard hooked the whip on his belt and pulled out a gun.

❏ ❏ ❏

It all took a while to absorb.

"So you mean that I switched places with my other self?" Dean Vanch asked Smit.

"That's correct," said Smit.

"My parents didn't die in carpet-bombing by the Francophones during the civil war?" Dean asked in amazement. "Collette was not shot during the ethnic cleansing? I wasn't sent to a labor camp because I broke the miscegenation laws by marrying a Francophone? My health is good because I didn't suffer from malnutrition during the Siege of Dieskau? I'm a wealthy man? And you even expect me to believe I don't need a passport to travel from California to Louisiana?"

"All correct," smiled Smit. "Are you happy now, Dean Vanch?"

"Are you kidding?" Dean asked. "If all you say is true, I'm the happiest man on Earth."

Comment on

"The Best of All Possible Worlds"

There's a saying: The optimist believes this is the best of all possible worlds. The pessimist fears this is true.

PUBLIC EYE

"**WANT TO GET OFF THE GRID,**" says the kid. Handle: "Monkey-C."

"Impossible," says the one-eyed man. Call him "Odin."

"Was told you could do it."

"No one escapes the Public Eye." Odin smiles. "Trick is to hide so's when the Eye looks right at you, it doesn't *know* it sees you."

"Show me," says Monkey-C.

"You know the first step."

Monkey-C knows. He plucks out his right eye—the cyborg implant that is actually a real-time camera linked to the net. His Public Eye. Everyone has one.

The grid is everywhere: in every stop light, ATM, subway, shopping mall, cash register, school, business, store-bought item, and in the right eye of every stranger, coworker, relative, or spouse. But Odin shows Monkey-C the tricks of the Invisibles. How to look to the grid like somebody else, like a piece of furniture, like a bot, like a blip. How to map a doppelganger to another part of the grid to throw off the Voyeurs. Months pass. Monkey-C learns well.

"Above all, have no friends," teaches Odin. "No enemies either. No family. No relationships of any kind. No one with a reason to *want* to see you."

"Harsh," says Monkey-C.

"Necessary," says Odin.

"Aren't we friends?"

"No."

Monkey-C plucks out his other eye, the left eye—also a camera. "It's recorded everything over the past months. My exposé of an Invisible."

"You," says Odin, betrayed. "Voyeur."

"Friend."

Monkey gives Odin the public eye and stumbles away, blind, smiling.

Comments on

"Public Eye"

In David Brin's novel, *Earth*, as well as in his non-fiction, he has discussed the worldwide destruction of privacy. In a transparent society, there might not be one Big Brother, but there are billions of Little Brothers, all ready to tattle on you. (I have a little brother and can relate). Robert Sawyer portrays a slightly more sympathetic transparent society in his trilogy, *Hominids, Humans* and *Hybrids*. The cybernetic implant that replaces an actual eye, is of course, a feature of Star Trek's lovable evil collective, the Borg.

This is another story that takes place in a world that I fleshed out a bit beyond what you see here. The story that follows, "Walker," takes place in the same universe.

Stylistically, I had fun with this piece. It was a bit of flash first published in *Winged Halo*. The word limit was 250 words, short even for flash, which forced me to snip fat. Given my tendency to wordiness, that's good practice.

WALKER

ON THE WAY HOME, as I passed the Chung Wah Funeral Home, I decided to turn off the patina in my Public Eye™. I have my favorite patinas—Ancient Rome, Underwater, Darkling Skies, and a couple I designed myself—but every now and then, I just like to see the world without any interface.

Incense scented the low drone of a Buddhist priest. Peeking through the open door, I could see him, in a saffron robe, at the head of a bier surrounded by red and white carnations. Two dozen mourners in white hoods crowded around the bier as well, doing something I couldn't see. Paper rustled in their hands, long tapers, which trailed ribbons of limpid smoke.

I turned the corner to walk up the street between the fire station and the freemasons lodge. The Walker stomped toward me. I knew him well by sight. Though he was the local homeless man, I could not recall if he had ever solicited money, and I wasn't sure he would accept it even if I offered. He always wore the same thing: jeans, toughened by many leagues of unwashed grime; a sweatshirt, which had once been white or light grey, but now matched the grunge dark of his pants; and an orange and khaki backpack, one of those tough, good quality packs hikers and trekkers use. Every time I saw him, he was walking. His face, worn, like his clothes, but equally tough, never looked unfocused. In this he was quite different from the other homeless person who haunted our neighborhood, the Lady With One Shoe. She was not only much filthier; she always looked like a survivor stumbling away from a suicide bombing in a subway, dusty and dead-eyed.

This was why I preferred to turn off the Public Eye™ every now and then. If I were looking at the Walker through the patina of Ancient Rome, he would have been blankface instead of in a toga, the Eye's way to let me know he was just a stranger, not on my friendlist. I never would have realized he was homeless, or dirty, or that I had seen him around a lot, always walking, walking, walking. A blankface is just a cipher in the patina. I'd never have noticed him.

I studied the Walker, glad to see him, really *see* him. I wondered where he had to go. Did he walk toward something or away? How many years of his life had he spent hiking back and forth through the city?

We were walking towards each other.

Oh, shit.

We were going to pass each other, and *his face wasn't blanked.* What happened if we made eye contact? It's one thing to gawk at someone from afar, but I wasn't ready to make contact with someone realtime who wasn't on my friendlist. And he would know I knew he was homeless, because I'd been staring at him with no patina, which was incredibly rude of me. Or maybe he wouldn't mind, but how would I know? I had no way to communicate with him, since I didn't know how to find him online. I mean, unless I spoke to him *directly.*

Should I try that? Should I smile and nod and murmur hello? Or avert my eyes and keep walking? Maybe it wasn't too late to turn my patina back on. But that felt cowardly.

I decided to go for it. I would meet his eyes directly and say, "Hi." I would do it, I really would.

He crossed the street in the middle of the block before he reached me, and kept walking, the same steady stride, past a fire hydrant, never looking back.

Comments on

"Walker"

Another flash, set in the same universe as *Public Eye*. In case you were wondering, there's a reason "Public Eye" is written differently here than in the first story. I wanted to show a tech device that, like Xerox or Google, started as a specific brand name, but became so ubiquitous that it turned into a common noun/verb. Monkey-C isn't the type to respect the sign posts of capitalism, and besides, his public eye is as much a part of him as the body parts he was born with, so trade marks aren't going to figure in his story. The uptight narrator of *Walker,* in contrast, sees his public eye less as a part of him than as a pop culture device he enjoys as a guilty pleasure. He also wants you to know that he has the top-of-the-line name brand, with several after-market upgrades, not some cheap rip-off from Senegal.

Public Eye is about the impossibility of invisibility in the twenty-first century, and how difficult it is to escape the grid, the scrutiny of billions. *Walker* shows the obverse: the impossibility of *escaping* invisibility, if you aren't a welcome part of the system. Sure, everyone might have a camera on 24/7, but who is to say they have to see what's really there? A camera does not just record reality, a camera fabricates fictions. The web connects us to everyone (who can afford it), yet it simultaneously segregates us into communities of people who all agree to look at the world in the same way.

Is technology really to blame? Did we have less privacy when we lived in hunter-gatherer bands or small villages and everyone knew everyone's business? Were we any less inclined to treat outsiders as invisibles?

Walker is a true story. It happens all the time, though no fancy tech is involved or needed.

A THOUSAND BLOSSOMS WITH THE DAY

10^{-8} seconds after the Big Bang

> *And look—a thousand blossoms with the day*
> *Woke—and a thousand scatter'd into clay;*
> *And this first summer month that brings the rose*
> *Shall take Jamshid and Kaikobad away.*

WHILE HE WAITED, he pondered what he would say to her. *The matter-antimatter annihilation burst will end, but my love shall forever endure...*

Oh, wonderful. Pretentious as well as tacky.

I know I don't deserve a sinistorsum like you, but I couldn't help loving you from the first moment my senses bombarded you...

So trite. Hardly an improvement.

Before he could think of something else, he felt a gentle patter of sensory bombardment on his back. He turned and there she was. He stared, openly barraging her like a blunt-sensed idiot. She was more beautiful than he remembered. The wordless pause stretched, and he could not stop pattering at her. He knew he should flash words at her, say something, *anything*, pretentious, tacky, trite, or downright idiotic--anything would be better than freezing up. But every careful phrase he had practiced flew right out of his mind.

"Deepshine," he blurted out her name, stupid, clumsy, a fool dextrorsum who never knew the right thing to say.

"Brightsharp." She rushed forward and merged her juncture with his. She had done it again, as only she could; she had made him feel that he had said just the right thing.

❑ ❑ ❑

They had met for the first time in Oppat Repository, three cycles ago.

She was there with a visiting group of students. Researchers of all kinds regularly toured the Repository, enabling the monks to share the latest developments in recovered or discovered knowledge. Brightsharp served as the group's guide to the huge building.

Though not yet a monk himself, Brightsharp had been raised in Oppat Repository. His sinistorsum twin had died in childhood, from Bleak's Syndrome, which meant that Brightsharp had little chance of retwinning in adulthood. Physically, he was capable, since there were treatments for the surviving twin of Bleak's Syndrome, but socially—that was another matter. In a more barbarous era, he would have been killed outright, from superstitious hate. In this age of renaissance, he had received the best education a child could want, right in the heart of the largest known Repository of the Ancients. It was understood he would become a monk.

He had never wanted any other life. Recovering and expanding the work of the ancients provided constant puzzles to solve, a giant game in which each victory of understanding over ignorance unfolded to reveal new mysteries. The monks were all post-adult dextrorsums or sinistorsums whose retwins had died, so they were solitaries, like Brightsharp. It seemed perfectly natural for him to follow in their footsteps.

Until he saw Deepshine.

The first stop along the tour was the Historium.

"Here the ancients preserved the history of our universe," Brightsharp explained to the group. They bombarded the display with a polite rain of interest. "Many of the storage strands containing the information were destroyed during the ages of barbarism, and many more decayed during the ages of neglect after the Repository was lost. But we have since been able to recreate much of what we think was stored there.

"The ancients discovered, and we have reconfirmed with modern science, that the universe is much, much older than a few hundred thousand generations, as was thought during the ages of barbarism. The time periods we deal with in cosmology are so vast that the ancients invented a new period of time called *seconds*, to measure it. One microsecond or 10^{-6} seconds, is equal to one trillion cycles. The universe itself began a little over one microsecond ago. Life has only existed for a few billion cycles. The entire evolution of sentience— our kind is the only known example we have yet discovered—is just a fraction of an era that itself lasts only a millionth of a 'second.'"

He felt a shy patter of attention on his body, and when he ventured a quick return volley of his own, he interlaced senses with a perfectly shaped sinistorsum. It was obvious from the jaggedness of her lateral juncture that she had only recently entered adulthood by separating from her childhood twin.

She flashed her name and a question.

"Deepshine here, sir. Could you explain how the monks know from the corpses of bursts that our universe is doomed? I've heard that but don't understand it."

It was a common question, one Brightsharp had answered glibly a dozen tours before. For some reason, he faltered this time as he flashed his reply.

"Uh, well, it isn't the only evidence. We, that is, the monks, I'm not really a monk, uhm..." He realized he was flashing directly at her. Embarrassed at his rudeness, Brightsharp diffused his focus back onto the whole group. "The energy of the burst, which our territorium depends upon for life, comes from the annihilation of quarks and antiquarks. The burst began to shine a few billion cycles ago, and it will continue to shine for few billion cycles, which is how long it will take the antimatter and matter inside the burst to annihilate each other. After the annihilation phase ends, a corpse of the burst will remain, made solely of matter. All the other of billions of bursts in space follow a similar lifecycle; the particles of our territorium, which are made of matter, were created from the remnants of such bursts. The reason is that there is a basic imbalance in the universe between the amounts of matter and antimatter quarks. We calculate that for every thirty million antiquarks there are thirty million and one quarks. What does it mean for life? It means that one day, every burst in the universe will sputter and die. All that will be left in space is a bare remnant of matter quarks. The universe is asymmetric."

"Asymmetric. Like you," wagged some wit from the back of the group.

A bitter pun, a clever insult; it evoked a ripple of laughter from the crowd at Brightsharp's expense. They looked no different than he did, solitary until they retwinned. They too, were asymmetric. But for them it would not be permanent.

Without meaning to, he darted a sensory volley at Deepshine. She did not jiggle with laughter. But neither would she return his tentative bombardment.

Brightsharp kept his words precise and professional.

"Furthermore, as it expands and cools, the universe will eventually lack enough heat or energy to maintain matter in the form that we know it. At a certain critical temperature, a first order phase transition will sweep across the universe. Matter itself, what piteous dregs remain, will freeze to death in a process called hadronization. The quarks that make up matter will no longer be able to maintain the massive high energy particles that enable the complex chemistry of life to exist. Quarks will freeze into lumps of two and three."

"The end of the universe," someone flashed.

"Not at all," corrected Brightsharp. "After the phase transition, the universe will endure, freezing cold, nearly empty, and eternally expanding, for more than $10^{10^{10}}$ seconds." He chuckled at the absurdity of that abysmal stretch of frozen dying. No one joined him. "Our lives register no meaning against the long eons of the universe."

A flash challenged him directly.

"I can't believe that." It was Deepshine.

❑ ❑ ❑

Alas that Spring should vanish with the rose!
That Youth's sweet-scented Manuscript should close!
The Nightingale that in the Branches sang
Ah, whence, and whither flown again, who knows?

Neither of them had planned to keep meeting one another. They were drawn against their better judgments. One secret rendezvous led to another. They had not intended to mingle junctures, but each tantalizing hint of how full retwinning would taste made it harder to stop. Finally, they realized they must make a choice, before biology made retwinning a mortal imperative. Retwin or stop seeing one another.

Brightsharp would not ask Deepshine to retwin. She had more to lose than he did. Social custom demanded that twins marry opposing twins, and Deepshine's twin, Shinedeep, already had in mind a match with a pair named Reachfar and Farreach. If Deepshine had had another pair of twins in mind, Shinedeep would consider them, but if Deepshine retwinned with Brightsharp, Shinedeep would be left single -- and shamed.

Deepshine declared that she was prepared to flout social custom to retwin with Brightsharp. They made an appointment to meet in one of their usual places. Once retwinned, they planned to flee the Repository, leave Oppat Territorium altogether, and settle in a distant territorium where no-one knew their history. Brightsharp knew he should talk her out of this folly, but instead he hurried through a garden of the Repository, on his way to retwin.

The immensity of what he was about to do suddenly overtook him, and he stumbled to a halt. He, Brightsharp, the twinless freak, was about to retwin. A sinistorsum wanted to join *him*.

Sharpbright, I wish you could be here to see this. It had been cycles since he'd allowed himself to think of his dead twin. Now he allowed the memories to return in full. Brightsharp drew in the patter of the garden: the wind blown tickle of the tufted herbs; the small, sharp probes of tiny floating things; the plodding zip-zap-zip-zap of a tube burrower nosing the tufts for food; the swirls of vagrant sensory interchanges churned into random whirlywigs by the wind. When Sharpbright died, a monk named Truelance had told Brightsharp that his twin would live on in a garden. The ancients had believed a literal garden awaited the dead, but modern monks taught a more subtle form of immortality consistent with science. After the complex particles making up a person disintegrated, they decayed into constituent particles. The tufts and tubes that fruited the territorium trapped and recollided these particles into heavier combinations, completing the circle. Sharpbright lived on in the elementary particles cycling through the changing patterns of life.

That had never been comfort enough before. After all, Brightsharp knew better than anyone that the seeming ability of life to reverse entropy was only an illusion, paid for in energy doomed to run out. The "circle of life" was actually better compared to a spiral, leading ever down. A "twist" of the spiral, whether breaking apart heavy particles into small ones or coalescing small particles into heavier ones, required a transition from one energy state to another. In heat equilibrium, no work was possible. The direction had to lead "down", to a lower state, because if there were no way to dump the excess heat generated by the work, the organism would fry itself. This had nothing to do with whether the work was being used to create heat or cold; a refrigeration device generated excess heat, in total, in order to create a localized area of coolness.

An organism could circle an infinite number of twists down the spiral only if it had access to an infinite tower of states. However, the cosmological constant, which the ancients had discovered must exist to explain the accelerating expansion of the universe, meant that there was a minimum temperature to the universe -- a bottom to the spiral. As long as life could operate above that temperature, life could subsist. Once the wavelength of thermal radiation grew larger than the size of the radiating system, no further cooling would be possible.

Even the Project could only delay the inevitable, not guarantee the survival of life and sentience. Brightsharp had devoted himself to the Project because it was all he had, not because it gave him true hope. Why scrabble after one more fraction of briefness when it could never be enough?

Ironic that only now he would have to leave Oppat Repository and the Project did he finally come to believe in its worth. If the Project could buy just one more cycle for sentience, it would be worth it. In fact, never before had he felt so greedy for time, time to grow old with Deepshine, time to lavish on the offspring he imagined them budding, time for their offspring to bud generation upon generation to come. The sweetness of the garden, the briefness of life: if it were part of *her*, it would be enough.

Was it Sharpbright's approval that Brightsharp felt wafting through the garden, or only his own happiness reflected back at him?

I'm already late. Deepshine will worry. Brightsharp forced himself out of the reverie. But he flashed at the garden before he left: *Thank you.*

□ □ □

> *Would you that spangle of Existence spend*
> *About the Secret—quick about it, Friend!*
> *A hair perhaps divides the False and True—*
> *And upon what, prithee, may life depend?*

Deepshine arrived at the rendezvous early, all her worldly possessions trimmed to fit in one small container. She felt a shuffle in the distance and sent a volley of sensory bombardment into the dimness. To her shock, the shape that approached her was not Brightsharp, but one of the monks.

Before she could concoct a likely excuse for her presence in this isolated corner of the Repository, the monk addressed her.

"I know who you are, and why you are here."

Deepshine quivered with shame and anger. "Do you?" she challenged. "Can you really understand?"

"I was young once," replied the monk. "We hoped that Brightsharp would give this up on his own, or that we could trust your sense of responsibility to your twin to restrain you to do what is right. But, obviously, we must intervene."

"There's nothing wrong with what we plan!"

"If you believed that, why would you scuttle about in secret, like vermin after scraps? No, child, you know what you propose to do is dishonorable. But perhaps you have not considered how it will harm Brightsharp -- and all of our species, if you continue with this selfish course."

"Harm Brightsharp?" she scoffed. "He is not a post-adult. It is harm to force him to live as though he were already one of you!"

"And you would be his salvation," sneered the monk. Deepshine recoiled at the blaze of his scorn. He made an obvious effort to gentle his next flashes. "Child, you have no idea who Brightsharp is. You cannot comprehend his needs."

"I will know once we retwin." They would become one.

"And by then it would be too late. We have raised twinless children here in Oppat Repository for hectocycles. Normally, the survivor of diseases such as Bleak's Syndrome leaves a survivor who is half a person, mentally retarded and socially incapable."

"That doesn't describe Brightsharp at all."

"No, it doesn't. Occasionally, a twinless displays something else, a form of intelligence just as abnormal, just as imbalanced, if you will, but of great value. Brightsharp's mind is such a mind. It is as if, being freed of the need to have a well-rounded personality, all that remains of his mind is focused on one kind of thinking, a deep mathematical kind of thought that surpasses the abilities of most people. None of the other twinless children in his generation have the capacity to share the work of the monks. Brightsharp not only can share in it, he contributes to it. He is vital to it. I do not think we will be able to finish the Project in time without him."

"I don't care."

"The future of our species depends upon it."

"What project could be so all-important?" demanded Deepshine.

"The survival of our people against the coming destruction. The Phase Transition."

Deepshine laughed uneasily. "Do not think me as ignorant as all that, monk! Brightsharp has spoken of it many times -- I know he is studying it -- and I know this 'Phase Transition' is billions of cycles in the future."

The monk pattered her hard, apparently trying to decide how much more to tell her. "By the time the temperature drops to the critical level that will trigger the phase transition, there will not be enough energy left for a civilization to draw upon to create the vehicle we need to survive the transition. The Phase Transition itself is far off, but our response to it must begin now. If we are not already too late."

"How could it be too late?" asked Deepshine. This paranoid vision of apocalypse repelled her, yet she found it hard to disbelieve entirely. Brightsharp had hinted... "Isn't there already a Ship?"

The monk flashed in anger, "He revealed that?" confirming what Brightsharp had only implied. "Yes, we have recovered a vehicle, if you can call it that, for it is larger than a thousand territoriums, left by the ancients. Already, kilocycles ago, they were preparing themselves for the inevitable. But their civilization fell before they could complete the Project. And we do not know how to finish the vehicle. To do that, we have to recapture the level of mathematics they used, especially concerning topological flaws. Brightsharp..."

"...isn't the only mathematical genius in the thousands of territoriums in the universe. He does not need to be part of your Project."

"He wants to be a part of it. He volunteered to be one of those to travel on the Ship. If he gives that up for you, a part of him will always regret it. Resent it. Repent it."

Shaken, Deepshine could not think of a reply.

"Did it never occur to you that perhaps seemingly bad things happen for a greater purpose?" the monk asked with glowing words, soft like prayers. "That Brightsharp was detwinned early for a purpose? A purpose greater than himself, greater than you, greater than all of us? Can you really compete with that?"

Deepshine fluttered a wan negative. Then, with a sob that wracked her body, she fled the Repository.

❑ ❑ ❑

When Brightsharp arrived, several microcycles later, he found the monk waiting for him in place of Deepshine.

"Truelance," Brightsharp said in surprise. "I... uh, was just..."

"She came and left," said Truelance.

"What?" he said, staring stupidly.

"She left a message. She could not bring shame upon her twin, Shinedeep. Child, I'm sorry. She hoped you would understand."

Brightsharp floundered in silence for a nanocycle, while the territorium turned summersaults in his gut. The universe laughed at him. "Yes. I understand."

❑ ❑ ❑

Strange, is it not? That of the myriads who
Before us pass'd the door of Darkness through,
Not one returns to tell us of the Road,
Which to discover we must travel too.

The assembly flashed and pattered politely as Brightsharp was introduced.

"Please welcome Brightsharp+Prosthetic, primary contributors to finding a viable solution to the Winwage+Holdwell's Paradox. Brightsharp+Prosthetic will be coordinating with the community leaders of Oppat to oversee the exodus to the Ship."

As a polite fiction, the introductory speakers referred to Brightsharp in the plural, as if he were retwinned. New technology had allowed Brightsharp to retwin with a prosthetic sinistorsum, which through biofeedback technology provided his mind with the illusion of a mirroring mind. Undoubtedly, it was a tremendous health breakthrough. But psychologically, his mind was not fooled. In his subjective experience of self, no amount of mental masturbation could compensate for his awareness of his own incompletion.

If only he had not flirted with the sensation of retwinning with Deepshine, the emptiness might not have stung so sharply. He wished he could curse her, hate her, blame her. But the prosthetic mirrored back his curses at him with echoes of the truth, that despite everything, he missed her, yearned for her and craved her.

Brightsharp ("plus Prosthetic," he thought wryly) explained to the crowd, as he had before, to many other groups, the solution to the Winwage+Holdwell's Paradox. Few of them could follow the math, but that was not the point. The point was to dazzle them.

This tour had not been his idea.

The truth was that the time for mathematicians and theorists had passed. The fate of the Project now lay with engineers and politicians, those who could master all the myriad details of calculation and coordination to conjunct billions of individuals with one great machine and one last hope. The monks had explained to Brightsharp that he could now best serve the Project by helping gather volunteers.

It wasn't easy. Even the scientists organizing the Project had to admit that ordinary life could go on for as long as another thirty microseconds. It was hard for ordinary people to work up a sense of urgency when the emergency was so far off. Brightsharp's job was to galvanize them. So after the brief dazzle of advanced mathematics, designed to convince them he was an expert worth listening to, Brightsharp began the spiel designed for him by the social engineers.

"I want to talk to you about the discoveries made by scientists in Gabeu and Hekint territoriums. Some of you may have heard of these discoveries already. The archeophysists there discovered that the stiches—the hypergates we all use to travel the huge distances between the bursts—could not have been made by our own ancestors, the Ancients.

"These stiches in spacetime were artificially made, we know that. But according to the solution of Winwage+Holdwell's Paradox, as I've just explained, the stitches must predate the Inflationary Period. The stitches are topological flaws in the fabric of spacetime that link one domain to another. Travel between domains would otherwise be impossible because they are further apart than the speed of light can travel.

"How is that possible? The only explanation is that life has arisen before; indeed that *intelligent* life has arisen before. In fact, this is predicted by the Mediocrity Principle..."

That was when he spotted them.

Although he had not seen Deepshine since she had retwinned, he recognized her right away. She had joined with an attractive dextrorsum. She looked good, retwinned.

Complete. Without him.

Brightsharp struggled to return to his speech.

"The Mediocrity Principle says that, statistically speaking, it is very unlikely that our species should have any privileged uniqueness. The universe, as we know it, is isomorphic and homomorphic, that is, the same in all directions with no privileged vantage point. This same rule should apply to life. Yet it seemingly does not: as far as we know, life arose only on one territorium and produced only one intelligent species. Of course, we quickly spread throughout the universe, so that within a short time of our evolution, the universe became homogeneous and isotropic with life. Our spread throughout the known universe may itself even be comparable to a first order phase transition. But have we really escaped the consequences of the Mediocrity Principle?

"Not at all. What we can conclude is that once life arises in a certain era, it will evolve enough intelligence to spread exponentially before any other form of life has time to evolve in that same era. Thus from its own vantage, it appears to be unique.

"But statistically speaking, that life is still 'mediocre' in terms of absolute uniqueness because life is statistically mandated to arise at least once and no more than once in any era which can support it. We are unique in space but not in time."

The audience pattered him unevenly, and Brightsharp knew many of them were confused. He avoided sensing Deepshine and her retwin.

"We term our era the Burst Era, because the heavens sparkle with bursts of exploding matter-antimatter. This is an era rich in energy, which enables more than a hundred kinds of particles to exist and create the complex chemistry of life. But we know our era will not last forever. The bursts will burn out when they have exhausted most of the antimatter in the universe. A phase transition will sweep over the universe, freezing the sparse remainder of quarks. Where once hundreds of particles were possible, now only a few limited particles will be stable: groups of three quarks will form protons and neutrons. Combinations of two quarks will make mesons. A few antiprotons, anti-neutrons and anti-mesons may also form, but those won't last long.

"But this hadronziation will not have been the first phase transition the universe has experienced. A previous phase transition, marked by the decoupling of the Electroweak force, began our era. Before that, the decoupling of the strong force from the electroweak force provided the energy needed to drive the inflation of the universe. In all, we would say that there are at least five major eras preceding our own. Each possessed a higher order of energy than the era that followed it. The earliest we can speculate about was the Planck Era, at the energy scale of M_{Planck}, which ended with the decoupling of gravity from the other forces. That was followed by the GUT Era, at the energy scale of M_{GUT}, which ended with the decoupling of the strong force, goading inflation. Then there was the era of Supersymetry, at the energy scale of M_{SUSY}, which ended with the breaking of supersymetry; the Electroweak Era, at the scale of 100 GeV; and finally, our own era, which operates at the energy scale of a mere 100 MeV.

"And in all of them, there was life."

❏ ❏ ❏

Finally, he had their attention.

"It was not life as we know it," Brightsharp explained. "The universe was far too hot and dense for our kind of life to exist, and the particles that create our chemistry didn't even exist yet. But according to the Scaling Hypothesis, at any given temperature, there is a form of life that can thrive at that temperature. The rate at which the lifeform uses energy, *and thus the rate at which it experiences consciousness*, is in direct proportion to its temperature. So beings that lived at a temperature twice as hot as ours would operate twice as fast, and think twice as fast. Beings which lived at temperatures a thousand or a billion or a trillion times as high as ours, as in the eras under discussion, would respectively experience vitality and consciousness by a factor of a thousand, a million, or a trillion times that of our own. For them, one nanocycle would be the equivalent of billions of cycles for us."

A rowdy pair of retwins in the back flashed a challenge: "If there were living beings before us, what happened to them all? Where are they?"

"Dead," Brightsharp answered. "All dead. Undoubtedly, they were as intelligent as we are. Undoubtedly, they had scientists who could peer into the past and predict the future, as we can. Undoubtedly, their civilization spanned their universe, as ours does.

"And undoubtedly, they were as reluctant to face the truth of their findings as we are.

"We believe that it was the GUT Era beings who created the stitches in hyperspace. They knew the inflation was coming, and that it would cause the universe to expand faster than the speed of light, forever separating their civilization into incommunicado domains. They exploited naturally forming topological defects to create a system that would leave links between the domains even after inflation. Even today, we can't fully comprehend how they achieved it.

"Yet for all their skill and wisdom, they failed at one thing. They failed to survive. They could foresee inflation, and obviously planned to live past it, yet they failed. We don't know why. But probably it was because by the time they finally grasped that the end was close, it was already too late.

"We don't want that to happen to us. That's why I'm before you this centicycle to beg you to consider volunteering to join the Ship that will travel into the future..."

❑ ❑ ❑

Deepshine+Reachfar awaited the dispersal of the small mob of the curious and the suspicious who pattered Brightsharp + Prosthetic after the lecture. Deepshine+Reachfar had hoped that retwinning would mellow the intensity of regret they felt for having lost Brightsharp. Strangely, it did not. They had a nagging sense that they were less, somehow, than they could have been. Yet, they told themselves, Brightsharp+Prosthetic had done well without them.

Only when Brightsharp+Prosthetic were alone did Deepshine+Reachfar finally approach them. For a moment, the retwins feared that Brightsharp+Prosthetic would not speak with them at all.

So Deepshine+Reachfar came right to the point. "We want to join the Ship!"

It was nearly comical. Brightsharp+Prosthetic had clearly expected anything but that.

"Wh...wha... what?" they sputtered.

"Isn't that what you are here for? To recruit volunteers in the prime of life?"

"Of course, but.... Listen, have you thought this through?"

"For many cycles." Deepshine had dreamed of it since before she had retwinned, since leaving Brightsharp. So strong had her desire been that now they both felt it as their own.

"No. No, I don't think it's a good idea," Brightsharp+Prosthetic said. "I'm sorry. I must turn you away."

Deepshine+Reachfar noted that Brightsharp referred to himself in the singular, a curiosity they found telling and sad.

"We think the Project will find us well qualified," they insisted.

"It's not that."

They bristled. "Brightsharp+Prosthetic, are you turning us away because of our previous personal encounter?"

Brightsharp+Prosthetic rippled with embarrassment. "No! Don't be absurd. I just don't want you to be taken in by a speech designed by social engineers to convince you to take a huge, foolhardy risk."

Deepshine+Reachfar felt an internal conflict. Deepshine felt mostly sadness, for the Brightsharp she remembered had not been a hypocrite. Reachfar, however, wanted to know what risk Brightsharp referred to beyond the obvious. After a brief rumination, they reached synthesis of their thoughts.

"We thought you believed in this Project, Brightsharp+Prosthetic," they said slowly. "What do you know that you did not tell the crowd?"

"The speech is not designed to emphasize the risks, that's all. But there are several. First is the process itself. The ship is a kind of deep freezer. In order to survive the hadronziation phase transition, we must cool and store our bodies in a form that has greater stability even than the frozen conglomerates of protons and neutrons that I mentioned in the lecture. This form of matter, called *strange matter* because of the percentage of strange quarks, is stable enough in large quantities to outlast the phase transition. But transferring our bodies into that state, the so-called 'packing process' is not easy, and the chance of death, for one retwin or both, is very high."

"We know this already," Deepshine+Reachfar said impatiently. "We familiarized ourselves with the Project's parameters before we made our decision. We are not fools."

"And what did you discover about the *unpacking* process?"

Deepshine+Reachfar rippled uneasily. They couldn't remember anything specific about unpacking, simply that it would occur a safe period of time after the phase transition had passed.

Brightsharp+Prosthetic laughed cynically. "You did not discover anything about it because we have no idea how to do it. Do you understand? Once we are packed, we don't know how to unpack ourselves! It's as if we plan to go to sleep with no way to wake up."

"But that makes no sense," Deepshine+Reachfar said, bewildered. "You must have some plan. Otherwise, what is the point of the entire Project?"

"The Project turns on a hope. Remember what I said about the Scaling Hypothesis, that life can exist in different eras characterized by different temperatures? Well, since we know that was true for the past, we are gambling that it is also true for the future. We are risking our whole civilization on the chance that in the far future, beings immensely slower and colder than we will evolve their own lumbering form of sentience. It is they we are depending on to unpack us."

"But that... that's insane!" Deepshine+Reachfar sputtered.

"Yes," laughed Brightsharp+Prosthetic. "Quite."

For a moment, Deepshine+Reachfar did consider backing out. But then, they shared the thought that they had known right from the start that the premise of the Project was crazy. Nothing had really changed.

"We still want to join," they said firmly. Nor could anything else that Brightsharp+Prosthetic said to them change their mind.

At last, seeing they would not budge, Brightsharp+Prosthetic gave in, whispering, "In truth, I envy you. To just once glimpse the future would be worth having endured the past."

"But you will be on the Ship too," they said. This unspoken assumption had been lurking under their determination all along, a hidden thought-stream of Deepshine's love.

"No." Brightsharp+Prosthetic bombarded them in surprise. "I thought you understood. Only those in their prime, who are both physically and mentally sound, will be allowed to carry our race into the future. And I, despite my prosthetic...." He shrugged; only now did Deepshine+Reachfar truly understand that he was still a solitaire despite the prosthetic. And she who had been Deepshine knew that by not retwinning with him, she had not given the Project as a gift to Brightsharp, as she had sacrificed her own happiness to do.

She had ensured that it would be forever out of his reach.

❑ ❑ ❑

And we, that now make merry in the Room
They left, and Summer dresses in new bloom
Ourselves must we beneath the Couch of Earth
Descend, ourselves to make a Couch—for whom?

There was after all one last task requiring Brightsharp's mathematical talents, and this was all that kept him from a downward spiral of dissipation and self-abuse. What he had told Deepshine+Reachfar was correct: there was no way for those packed in strange matter to unpack themselves. But there were ways that they could increase their chances of being noticed by the "Coldslows+Slowcolds" —the hypothetical lifeforms of the future. Others were working on a signaling method. Brightsharp's job was to find the best time to emit the signal.

According to the Scaling Hypothesis, all other factors being equal, for every temperature there was a lifeform able to thrive at that temperature. However, all other factors were not equal. The grinding force of entropy sent time spiraling downward, ever downward, in a finite plunge towards lower and lower available scales of energy. The universe was not homogeneous through time, and all eras were not equivalent.

What mattered more than the absolute amount of energy available was what degree of work the "chemistry" allowed by that amount of heat could accomplish in the given span of time available before the steady drop in the temperature of the universe made that "chemistry" obsolete. Brightsharp's kind of life was lucky. The light of the bursts along with the residual warmth left from the Big Bang kept quarks swimming around energetically enough to form a whole zoo of various particles from which to combine and recombine into living forms. The effective complexity of potential life was determined by total time for evolution, the available power output, the temperature scale, and the subjective length of consciousness that resulted. It had taken life billions of cycles to emerge in the Burst Era, and life might freeze to extinction megacycles before the arrival of the dreaded phase transition. Thus, in this era at least, there was only a short window of effective complexity. Probably that had been true for the lifeforms from previous eras as well.

Within certain windows of opportunity, the universe would give rise to life, to intelligence, with clockwork inevitability. But those precious windows were as islands in an archipelago separated by a vast and empty sea.

According to Brightsharp's calculations, the next window of effective complexity would not occur for more than 3×10^{17} seconds: trillions and trillions of cycles.

He did not know why the picture of those trillions of cycles yawning between him and the future awakening of the Ship should drive him to despair.

Because Deepshine will cross that gulf without you, a taunt bounced back at him from the mirror mind of his prosthetic.

Oh. Yes.

He gave up work on the problem and went back to dissipation and self-abuse.

❑ ❑ ❑

> *Oh if the World were but to re-create,*
> *That we might catch ere closed the Book of Fate,*
> *And make the Writer on a fairer leaf*
> *Inscribe our names, or quite obliterate!*

"There has been a terrible accident," Greatglow+Findwise flashed in clear distress. "We thought you would want to know because the retwin was one of your recruits—Deepshine+Reachfar."

Brightsharp felt as though his constituent quarks had frozen into hadrons a trillion cycles too soon. Within three centicycles, he had made the eight stitch jump to Hekint territorium, where the packing process for the Ship was in progress.

There Project administrators somberly explained that one of the retwins had perished during complications in the packing. Brightsharp insisted on visiting the survivor in the hospital.

When Brightsharp entered the annex to the hospital room, the doctor bombarded him with careful scrutiny.

"Ah," said the doctor. "Excellent. So they were able to find another candidate in need of a new retwin. I feared they would not be able to find someone willing to retwin only to retry this damned packing process."

Dumbfounded, Brightsharp followed the doctor into the hospital room.

A sinistorsum lay in the recovery sling.

Deepshine.

For a moment, Brightshine knew only overwhelming relief. Then suddenly, what the doctor had said sank in. Tragedy had ironically led him to what he had dreamed of for so long. He could twin with Deepshine at last.

Except – she had rejected him. How could he join with her, integrating into himself forever the contempt that had led her to betray his trust those many cycles ago?

"You're having doubts," the doctor flashed.

"I just ... need to think. Can I be alone?" Brightsharp asked.

The doctor said nothing, only directed Brightsharp to a door that opened on a garden. But Brightsharp could still feel the unflashed disappointment.

Of course you can be alone, his prosthetic reflected his own thought back at him. *It is being with another that you have never managed.*

In the small hospital garden, Brightsharp paced and probed the deep well of bitterness that had grown up inside him in the past cycles without his even being aware of it. When had his love for Deepshine turned into hatred? Or had he come to despise himself so deeply that now he was willing to drag her down with him just to have the pleasure of destroying himself? His prosthetic had not tempered the hidden knots of his wounded pride, it had only amplified them. He laughed bitterly at himself. A slight flaw in the design, no doubt—but was the flaw in the prosthetic or in himself?

Tufted herbs tickled him with their soft, vegetative pitter-patter. He let the meaningless flashes drift over him, gradually calming his agitation. He kept still for a long time.

Out of nowhere, he suddenly found a mathematical solution to the problem he had been working on before his binge of self-sabotage. There it was, the exact calculation for the next period of effective complexity. Like a tufted flower, the solution bloomed in his mind, simple, elegant, complete. He could predict within a period of 10×30^{15} seconds exactly when intelligent life would evolve.

In the same stunning moment, it hit Brightsharp that the only way his species would meet with another sentient species was if the Project worked. Any sentient species that arose within its window of opportunity was destined to spread so quickly through the universe that it usurped any potential competition. Only if a civilization found a way to cross the empty ocean between islands of opportunity would a conference of sentient minds be possible.

Perhaps they will not like us; perhaps they will despise or hate us. Or perhaps we will find that they have been as lonely as we. Perhaps they have answers we have not dreamed of, or perhaps they are baffled by the same questions as we are. But no matter what they are like, just to meet them, just to know them, it would be worth it....

Just to meet her, just to know her, it would be worth it, *his prosthetic echoed him back to himself.*

He felt something tip-tap-tip-tap at him, and realized that a small tube burrower had mistaken him for a tuft.

"I'm sorry, my friend," Brightshine smiled. "I'm not ready to re-join the garden just yet."

He returned to the room where his retwin awaited him.

> *And fear not lest Existence closing your*
> *Account and mine, should know the like no more;*
> *The Eternal Saki from that Bowl has pour'd*
> *Millions of bubbles like us, and will pour.*
>
> *(The Rubaiyat of Omar Khayyam)*

Comments on

"A Thousand Blossoms With the Day"

I know a lot of you finished this story thinking, "You know what this story needs? More physics." Well, you can have your wish.

This is very much an idea piece. Although I'm a liberal arts major, I like to read physics papers. I skip the math and just read the words. (My brother, a physicist, reads the same papers, but he skips the words and reads just the math.) One day I chanced to be enjoying Freeman Dyson's infamous paper, "Time Without End: Physics and Biology in an Open Universe," (*Reviews of Modern Physics*, Vol. 51, No. 3, July 1979) along with several other papers debating the problems with it. For instance, Katherine Freese and William H. Kinney, at the Michigan Center for Theoretical Physics, University of Michigan, argued in their paper, "The ultimate fate of life in an accelerating universe," that life cannot go on indefinitely in a universe dominated by a cosmological constant. *The Five Ages of the Universe: Inside the Physics of Eternity,* by Fred Adams and Greg Laughlin, was another book that intrigued me.

That's when the story idea hit me. Of course, my idea was for a novel (as always), but divided into short stories about each major "era" in the life of the universe. The novel would also have humans.

Here's the key passage from Dyson's paper:

(i) Is the basis of consciousness matter or structure?

...Let me spell out more explicitly the meaning of question (i). My consciousness is somehow associated with a collection of organic molecules inside my head. The question is, whether the existence of my consciousness depends on the actual substance of a particular set of molecules or whether it only depends on the structure of the molecules. In other words, if I could make a copy of my brain with the same structure but using different materials, would the copy think it was me?

... Since I am a philosophical optimist, I assume as a working hypothesis that the answer to question (i) is "structure". Then life is free to evolve into whatever material embodiment best suits its purposes.

The first consequence is that the appropriate measure of time as experienced subjectively by a living creature is not physical time t but the quantity

$$u(t) = f \, INT(0,t) \, theta(t') \, dt',$$

where theta(t) is the temperature of the creature and $f = (300 \deg \sec)^{\wedge}(-1)$ is a scale factor which it is convenient to introduce so as to make u dimensionless. I call u "subjective time". The second consequence of the scaling law is that any creature is characterized by a quantity Q which measures its rate of entropy production per unit of subjective time. If entropy is measured in information units or bits, and if u is measured in "moments of consciousness", then Q is a pure number expressing the amount of information that must be processed in order to keep the creature alive long enough to say "Cogito, ergo sum". I call Q the "complexity" of the creature. For example, a human being dissipates about 200 W of power at a temperature of 300 K, with each moment of consciousness lasting about a second. A human being therefore has $Q = 10^{23}$ bits.

Basically, creatures with a great deal of energy (heat) available to them would think and live at a much more accelerated pace than humans. Creatures with a great deal less energy (colder) would operate slower. In theory, life could exist long after the stars had all burned themselves into cold, distant black holes. By the same token, it could exist at the extremely high temperatures that existed right after the Big Bang, when more than 99% of the matter and antimatter particles in the universe interacted and annihilated one another. Hundreds of exotic particles, which today exist only in particle accelerators, swam in a hot soup. In this story, I hypothesize that the matter-antimatter "bursts" are as suns to the creatures who regard the end of the bursts with the same horror that we regard the death of all the stars.

Originally, this story had the mischievous subtitle, "a historical romance."

I wrote this in 2003, and I realize research into the early universe has marched on. Also—liberal arts major here. If I've flubbed the science or there's some updated theory I should know about, feel free to email me and let me know: tara (at) taramayastales (dot) com. I'm still working on the novel, so I welcome the chance to make corrections and improvements.

YOU HAVE NOT FORGOTTEN HOW TO FLY

YOU PLACE THE GLOP of scratchy mush onto your first and second fingers and wiggle it on a flight path toward the toddler.

"Here comes the faery, flying into your mouth! Zo-zo-zoooooom-za!"

He watches you with a wide-open O of a mouth until the moment you are about to stick the fingerlick of food in his mouth. Then his jaws clamp shut, sealed by a thin line of pressed lips.

You are trying to persuade the baby of the merits of corn mush. This is all the more difficult because you have your doubts about corn mush yourself. In fact, you have profound reservations about corn mush. You can't stand the texture—you prefer smooth purées to mushes or mashes of any sort—and frankly, the color repels you. Food ought not to be such a bright yellow. Deep orange like squash, yes, or a regal green like spinach, certainly. And why is it that every kind of food made from corn must be scratchy? Corn bread is scratchy, corn mash is scratchy, even popped corn is scratchy. You never used to eat corn, and you still aren't too fond of it. This is difficult, because corn is the staple of your husband's people. They eat corn with every damn thing.

While you are musing about your loathing for the food you're trying to feed the baby, he reaches up and knocks the glop of corn right off your hand. It lands on the floor.

"No want eat!" He waves little fists to emphasize his resolve.

"Never mind," you tell him. "It doesn't matter. There's more. I have a whole bowl. See?"

You show him the bowl as you set it down on the adobe platform beside the mat where he sits—out of his reach, so he doesn't spill any more.

The floor is adobe, whitewashed frequently to fight the smoky residue from the beehive shaped oven in the corner of the room. The bright yellow glop shows up startlingly bright against the white. You hurry to find a broom, to sweep away evidence of the spill, before your husband sees it.

Unfortunately, this is when your husband pushes aside the tapestry of painted and plaited reeds to enter the doorway to the kitchen. His eyes are immediately drawn to the spilled bite of corn on the floor, as a vulture would be drawn to carrion.

His face purples with rage. "Boy! Did you throw food again?"

"No want eat!" the toddler shouts back. No doubt about it, he's his father's son.

Agonized by this squander, your husband bends down and carefully scoops up the corn mush from the floor. *No*, you tell yourself, *he won't*, but he does. He tries to shovel the corn from the floor into your son's mouth.

The toddler will have none of it. Although he is only a third the size of the man trying to feed him, the baby seems endowed with the strength of ten men and the stubbornness of twenty. He thrashes his head side to side, his whole face scrunched shut, so even his cheeks and eyebrows and bright red ears appear to help his mouth repel the rejected food.

"Do you know how lucky you are to have this food!" bellows your husband. "Do you know how many good people could have survived the famine if they'd had the food you just threw away!"

"NO WANT EAT!" your son screams back.

The minute his mouth is open, your husband thrusts the food in. "Fa! No one under my roof will waste food!"

The baby spits the corn mush back into his father's face. You marvel at the ghastly revelation that spit up corn mush *looks exactly the same* as regular corn mush. But you can see that having corn spit in his face has pushed your husband past the boundary of sage thought. He heaves himself up, wipes the corn from his face, still careful to save as much of it as he can in the shelter of his palm, and says in a terrible voice, "YOU WILL EAT THIS!"

He is about to try to shove the much-abused mush into the toddler's mouth when you fling yourself between man and baby.

"Stop it!" you shout. You don't want to shout, but you have to, just to make yourself heard. "Leave him alone! He doesn't have to eat the wretched stuff if he doesn't want it."

Your husband is about to hit you. He will smack you out of the way and then attack your son, shoving the hated mush down his throat. But he meets your eyes, and some part of him remembers you are not an ordinary mortal woman, resigned to such treatment. You are a faery. You have wings, and though you have folded them behind you, out of use, you have not forgotten how to fly. Some part of him remembers that he is the hero who overthrew a tyrant, and being a true hero, he is not the kind of man who hits his wife or child. Or perhaps he is thinking something else entirely, but either way, he lowers his raised fist. His whole body snaps back. He's still angry, so he leaves the room.

You sag next to your son. Because of the oven, the kitchen is always sweltering; the fumes sting your eyes. You want to leave the room yourself, to fly away on a cool breeze and release the tension in your body. Maybe shed a tear or two. It's been a long day, and you realize you hate this kitchen, which always smells of burnt corn. But someone has to stay with the baby.

"Mommy!"

You ignore him. You are on the floor next to the adobe platform where your son sits. With your wings folded behind you, you can lean back against the dais. You're too tired to fight with your chubby baby over food. You don't care if he eats. It won't bring back the dead. Does your husband think he is the only one who has lost family? You lost your entire race. You are the last. Does he ever remember that?

"Mommy! Mommy!" Your toddler tugs at your wing, which is all he can reach from where he sits on the adobe dais. "Mommy! I want eat."

You crick your neck. "What?"

"I want eat!"

You hand him the bowl, and watch in amazement as he happily shovels the whole bowl of yellow mush into his mouth.

Comments on

"You Have Not Forgotten How To Fly"

This piece is an extract from my fantasy epic series, *The Windwheel and the Maze*. Don't worry—or don't get your hopes up, depending on how exotic your tastes are—the main story line is written in third person, past tense; but there are several storylines at work in each book, intertwined. At one point in the series, we encounter a faery, immensely old and powerful, who has married a mortal. She has been Cursed by Lady Death, and is slowly losing her memories, so she desperately tries to hold on to them by reminding herself of the important moments in her life, told in second person, present tense. Meanwhile, the heroine, Dindi, is trying to save her, but the tribes who need to stand united against Lady Death are busy fighting a war against one another.

The Windwheel and the Maze series began as a book called *The Rainbow Dancer*. I started it in 2000, when I worked night shifts at the homeless shelter. As I mentioned in the comments on *Ghosts on Red Strings*, I joined the Online Writing Workshop for Science Fiction, Fantasy, and Horror. My great opus, *Avatars of the Archons*, had been rejected (by one publisher) and I took this as a Sign that my writing sucked. I needed to learn how to write, I decided. The solution: write a "practice" novel. It would be a standard fantasy, with standard tropes, nothing special. Its only purpose in existing would be for me to hone my craft. I expressly forbade myself to fall in love with the story, as I had fallen in love with my epic, or to waste five years on it, as I had wasted five years on my epic.

I *did* fall in love with the story, and I ended up spending *ten* years on it.

There is one advantage in writing a book/series over a long period, which is that the work grows with you. This tale braids together several intertwined plotlines. The main story line, which I wrote first, is a Coming of Age story. It follows a fairly conventional fantasy trope of a young person coming into her power and falling in love. Another strand of the story, however, follows another couple (a generation older), and their story serves as a counterpoint to the main story. It is about Coming of (Older) Age, about marriage rather than courtship, and about learning, sometimes, to give up power.

It's probably no accident that in the intervening decade since I began the story, I settled down, married, and started a family.

DELIVERY STATUS NOTIFICATION (FAILURE)

STOIC, I THINK. *My character needs to be stoic.*

I wrote half the scene on my laptop but to finish it I must email it to myself on my main computer. For some reason, each time I Send, I end up with a *Delivery Status Notification (Failure)*. In the middle of my third *Delivery Status Notification (Failure)*, my mother calls.

"What's going on with the swim lessons?"

I've put off this conversation two days. I try to explain about the cost of gas, the distance to her house, the other pool option. She doesn't want to hear it.

"He just doesn't want your kids to spend time with their grandmother," she complains.

I email the attachment to a different address. This time it works. My file fills my screen. I put my cell on speakerphone so I can type without interrupting my mother. She is working out a number of different alternative schedules. Tuesdays and Thursdays or Wednesdays and Fridays, eight or ten o'clock, private or class lessons. I surf the net while she talks. From Epictetus, via Wikipedia, I learn to be stoic is to be "sick and yet happy, in peril and yet happy, dying and yet happy, in exile and happy, in disgrace and happy." How should I show this in my character? Show, don't tell, show don't tell.

The half-written scene is a mess, a number of mutually conflicting scenelets, bits of possible dialogue. Should I put in a flashback? Or would that drag the pace? I realize I don't know if my character has parents or is an orphan. It's always easier to deal with a character who is an orphan. Parents just complicate fiction. Parents, like flashbacks, seldom move the plot forward.

"Are you listening to me or are you on the computer?" my mother asks.

"I'm trying to work."

"I know you're trying to work," she says, "but we need to get these swim lessons taken care of. Why do they need to be at the same time?"

"What?" I realize she must have asked me a question before, and I must have given her an answer that has made her imagine I require something to be at the same time. "I don't know. I'm trying to work while the baby is still asleep. He'll be up from his nap soon."

"You're really annoying to talk to when you get like this," she says. "It's rude."

There's definitely a scenelet missing, a bit I wrote last night around two in the morning, while nursing the baby. I was sleepy, but I distinctly remember writing it, on my laptop. Damn. I emailed myself the wrong draft. I've been working on the wrong draft this whole time. I go back to my laptop to email myself the right draft.

The baby cries. I use this as an excuse to hang up. After I've changed the baby's diaper and started to nurse, I check my email again.

Delivery Status Notification (Failure).

Comments on

"Delivery Status Notification (Failure)"

There's something self-indulgent about writing about writing. Have you ever noticed how many protagonists of novels are writers, and how many protagonists of movies are actors? *Wow, you really reached there, didn't you Ms./Mr. Author/Screenwriter?* I promised myself I would avoid that cliché.

As you can see, I broke that promise. It's natural to write about writing because it's natural to write about oneself, and if one is a writer.... Well, there you go. It happens. I hope this flash piece is not *just* about being a writer, or even *mainly* about that.

I never sought formal publication for this piece; it just appeared on my blog. I didn't want to let it slip away into the blogoblivion of the archives, so I slipped it in here.

THE PAINTED WORLD:
DRAWN TO THE BRINK

A BRINK HAD ESCAPED from across the twixting, and when the glamourers drew colors, Sajiana's ribbon came up silver. With an extravagant sigh of resignation, she packed up her linen papers, her scribs and her knots, pretending to a reluctance to leave the stuffy halls of Mangcansten. Once loose upon the moor, with the grouse and the heather and the wind whip-a-man through her hair, she broke into a whistle. She trod no road, and needed none. Upon her back she carried her large, flat portfolio, her scribroll and a smaller rucksack of odds and ends. She pitied herself only because the brink had left a trail a first-year draftsprentice could have followed. In no time at all, she would have the creature's picture in a knot. Once she disposed of it, duty would force her back to dreary Mangcansten.

However, she was in no danger of overtaking the brink that day. When dusk came, she waited through the twixting time, then found a likely spot upon the empty moor to camp for the night. She had a folder of prepared etchings, including many of little cottages. Sajiana had a fine eye for detail. Even these simple sketches included whimsies such as ivy curled over the stones in the fireplace and watering cans sitting upon windowsills planted with radishes. She placed one drawing in the center of a flat expanse of sward, and then set out her knots at a distance around it. Three knots could serve, at minimum, but because Sajiana hunted a brink, she set out four for safety. As she tugged tight the last knot, the glamour caught the piece of paper. Picture billowed into reality. Now a cozy cottage, with potted radishes in the windows and a roaring fire puttering smoke from the ivy-covered fireplace, stood, snug as you like, before her.

The key to a good etching was to fill in the view through the windows. If you hinted at what lay inside, that sufficed. No need to draw *all* the insides separately, as long as enough showed in the picture for the glamour to operate upon it. In the same spirit, if one drew a picture of a cabinet, one must always draw one drawer open just enough to show something inside. Otherwise, when one opened the door of one's house, or the drawer of one's cabinet, one was apt to find a blank white interior.

In the windows of the cottages that Sajiana sketched, one always caught a glimpse of a snuggly bed on one side and a table laden with food on the other. When she opened the blue door to the cottage, therefore, she found a teakettle just coming to boil, a plate of scones, a hardboiled egg and breaded veal cakes. She tucked in with a will. Nothing like a day of walking to whet an appetite! She banked the fire and crawled into the warm bed.

Dawn *almost* caught her by surprise. It had been that long since she'd been on the road. She leaped out of bed just as the twixting of daybreak dissolved the knots on the glamour. As usual, once the glamour vanished, no sign of the piece of paper remained. Bed, table, fireplace, cottage, all misted into the morning fog and left Sajiana shivering in her nightclothes on the desolate moor. Grumbling under her breath, she scurried to her rucksack—no glamour—and pulled on her trousers and jacket of wool felt—no glamour either.

She shoved the nightdress into a crumpled lump in her sack and resumed her trek across the roadless moor.

Fourteen drawings later, she reached a town called Paddiglum. The brink had arrived here a few days ago, after taking a much more haphazard route that zigzagged across the moor. The brink would be hungry, and this one was too inexperienced – perhaps it was young – to know that it would do better to lurk out in the wilderness and waylay travelers than risk coming into a human town.

She could have drawn herself a dress of crimson silk, sewn with buckles and bells of gold and a tall moon shaped hat to match. However, Sajiana preferred the anonymity provided by her ragged, rugged, *real* travel clothes. She tromped through the town, whistling, past villagers dressed no better than she, ignoring and ignored. She had a string in one hand, a scrib and a slip of blank paper in the other. A close observer would have seen that the string did not dangle from her hand, but poked its head out this way and that, gently tugging at her fingers. These were the tugs that led her ever closer to the brink.

The string suddenly jerked her quite hard toward an alley along the cheesemonger's street. Sajiana looked up and met the eyes of a startled young man. His hair tousled about his head all unruly. His eyes were huge in his face, haunted. His lips pressed together under hungry cheeks. Strange that in all this time since he had escaped from the twixting, he had not used his considerable powers to better maintain himself.

Some brinks tried to run. Some tried to fight. The outcome would be the same. This brink looked at her a long moment, hard. He walked away. It was as though he lacked either the humility or the sense to fear her.

His striking face would be his undoing; she could hardly forget a face like that. Sajiana sat down against a wall beside a cheese shop. In feathery, charcoal strokes of her scrib, she began to sketch the face she remembered. It took her only a few minutes to have a likeness. It took her longer to tie the complex knot around the portrait. With her knotted portrait, Sajiana stood and walked into the alley.

"Come to me," she said.

She heard him before she saw him. A scritching and scratching and scrapping sound: he fought each step of the way to answer her call. He could not resist the compulsion, however, and he finally dragged himself into view. His eyes no longer looked haunted. They blazed with hate.

"You would dare draw *me*? Do you know who I am?"

"Just another brink, as far as I'm concerned," Sajiana said.

Whatever answer he had been expecting, it had not been that. He stared at her, flummoxed. "Are you mad? What are you talking about? I'm no brink!"

His surprise surprised her. She had never met a brink who did not know it was a brink. Most boasted of their inhuman superiority.

"Did you honestly think you were human?" she asked, overcome with curiosity against her better judgment. The teachers at Mangcansten universally advised against entering into prolonged discussion with a brink.

"I *am* human," he said. "And the fact you cannot bind me proves it."

He wrenched himself free of the compulsion. This time he did run.

The charcoal portrait had become a smudged mess of meaningless lines. She rolled a choice curse around the inside of her mouth. Because he had not attacked anyone, stolen anything, or wrecked any havoc, she had assumed him to be weak. Instead, it appeared he had a stronger will than any brink she had previously encountered. Sajiana began to worry that a more experienced glamourer should have been assigned to this brink. She had a quick hand, but not the patience for the truly intricate work needed to bind an extremely powerful will. The brink was wrong if he thought that humans could not be bound by a portrait. That was what humans and brinks had in common. However, a strong will could turn a line drawing to mush. She would have to put more effort into it.

She blew air between her teeth. She untied and unrolled her scribroll. It contained an assortment of scribs and brushes. She chose one of the thin charcoal scribs. She peeled back a layer of the wax paper to reveal more nub. She began to draw the brink again, this time his whole body. He wore a kora, a forward-curved sword that broadened at the tip. His cape-coat had once been elaborate but the clasps and bells had been torn off the indigo velvet. Beneath it, the blouse of white silk may once have been pristine. Most brinks were painted richly adorned. However, why had he let the garments wear down to near rags?

"Glamourer!" a cheery shout interrupted Sajiana's concentration. Annoyance soured the smile she flashed to the man who had interrupted her with his salutation. She reminded herself that Mangcansten was surprisingly intolerant of punching locals in the face.

"Glamourer!" He was a portly man, balding, richly belled in silk, with a moon shaped hat that protruded like a horn from the center of his head. Gold clappers cupped his ears, and bangles jingled on his thick wrists. He was seated in an open veyance drawn by massive Tugger hounds. "What an honor to meet one of your mastery! What brings you here to our remote hamlet?"

"Our business need not worry you," she replied coolly. So that no one could see her drawing a forbidden human form – though if he knew she was a glamourer, he would know she had the right – Sajiana filed the paper and scrib back into her portfolio.

"But you must let us assist you. I am the town Honorary, Lord Master Yorch. Have you a place to stay? Oh, I know you glamourers have your own ways of providing shelter, but surely you will permit me the vanity of offering you the hospitality of my house."

Sajiana sighed and gave in to the inevitable. Perhaps it would be better to work on the portrait of the brink inside, on a flat surface, with good light. She climbed up beside Lord Master Yorch and allowed him to babble at her the rest of the trip to his large mansion. She would have to resume her hunt for the brink later.

Most of the houses in Paddiglum were lumped from stone, but Lord Master Yorch's mansion was a warm amber jewel of carven woods. Soldiers in serviceable brown cape-coats and iron helmets stood watch inside the house. A lovely, yet listless maid showed Sajiana to a guest chamber.

Sajiana pleaded fatigue and hid in the guest chamber until supper. The sun set; she lit lamps. She drew and burned several drafts of the brink's portrait. None were true enough to hold him, and there was no point in knotting him just to let him escape again. After a frustrating afternoon, she decided to allow herself to doodle to clear her mental palette before she tried again. She set aside the fine linen canvas she had been working and took out her sketchbook. She always liked to practice upon real rooms, and she especially liked to look at the insides of things because without those views, a picture would lead to a poor glamour. Much heavy oaken furniture adorned the guest chamber. Sajiana sketched the bed, then the casement window and the bronze grill across it, then a clever chest at the foot of the bed, and then a large dresser against the far wall. She opened one drawer...

...Inside it was quite blank. White.

Shocked, Sajiana stared at it a minute. Then she checked under the bed. White. Behind the curtains on either side of the window. White. Inside the chest in the corner. White....

Was it possible? How? The mansion had not vanished at sunset...

"Ah, yes, sorry, this room still has some rough spots," a mocking voice lamented.

Sajiana whirled to face the man in the doorway. Lord Master Yorch.

"I suppose it was only a matter of time before Mangcansten sent someone to investigate," he said. "But the scribblers of Mangcansten are not the only ones who know how to knot a portrait."

He lifted his hands, revealing a painting of a woman. Water colors, hasty and slapdash, they would be possible to escape, except that he had a true talent for capturing detail. He had caught the curve of her neck, the shape of her brow, the way strands of her hair fell across her face.

Sajiana cried out and ran toward him, but she knew even before she felt the searing jab of pain that she would not stop him before he finished the knot around the painting of her. She stumbled to her knees just in front of him. He laughed softly. He reached out and tipped her chin up, forcing her face to tilt to his scrutiny.

"You're pretty enough, and a man tires of paper women. Perhaps I will keep you on my string a while before I end you, glamourer. Take off those rags."

She could feel the binding on her mind, chaining her to his will. Powerless in her rage, she obeyed him.

"Draw a gown for yourself," he said. "And join me for supper."

Though he left, the compulsion to obey him remained. She reminded herself that watercolors were not oils. She should be able to squirm free. However, it would take many weeks filled with long hours of concentration. And he would be most alert for any attempts tonight. So she did as she had been bid. Black silk. Gold bells. Scarlet hat.

The drawing and knotting took her only moments. However, she did not stop. She pulled out of her portfolio another sheet of paper, one of the best quality weave.

Once more, she began to etch the brink.

Perhaps danger honed her concentration. Perhaps the helpless hate that boiled in her helped her to catch the glint of that same emotion in the eye of the brink. The shape that formed under her charcoal nib was truer than any she had ever been able to draw. She tied on the knot, looping each strand with utmost care. When she had finished, she hid the package back in her portfolio.

She could feel Lord Master Yorch tugging at her will, demanding her presence downstairs.

"Come to me," she whispered to the empty room.

All through the farce of dinner, Sajiana sat stiffly by Lord Master Yorch's side while he played the role of genial host. He had several guests, town magistrates and their wives, a few merchants, a guild master. None of them appeared aware that the glamourer who was the guest of honor had actually been imprisoned in the vilest way by her host. The oblivious laughter and meaningless chatter of the other guests made Yorch's knowing smirks all the harder to bear.

She puzzled over the mystery of Yorch's power. He had knotted a glamour, but tied it to what? Why did the mansion not disappear when it crossed the twixting times of dusk and dawn?

Sajiana saw no sign of the brink. He must have come to the room where she had commanded his presence, and, in her absence, willed his way free of the drawing. As she gave the matter deeper consideration, she felt relief. She didn't know why she had drawn the brink. If Yorch had left her with her scribs and sketchbooks, it was because he knew that as long as he controlled her, he controlled her magic. The last thing she wanted to do was deliver a brink to him.

❑ ❑ ❑

"Come with me," Lord Master Yorch said to Sajiana after the listless servants took away the dinner. She followed him up the main stairs, across the hall, and up a back stair that she had not noticed before, to the third floor.

"Take off your clothes," he said. He put a key to the heavy door at the top of the stair. "You won't need them for what I have in mind."

Sajiana dropped off the gown. As it fell away, it turned back into a sheet of paper, with the drawing jumbled into uselessness.

Behind the door lay a painting studio.

One huge oil painting, canvas mounted on a wood frame, dominated the room. Sajiana recognized Yorch's mansion. Years of detail had gone into every minute stroke of the painting. Each room could be seen through the large windows. People, servants and soldiers, could be seen in the rooms. Lord Master Yorch exchanged his cape-coat and the sword belted at his waist for a painter's smock.

He pointed to a couch. "Recline."

Step by step, Sajiana's feet forced her to the divan. She was re-minded of the scritching walk of the brink when she had called him in the ally. She did not enjoy the irony of being on the other side of the knot.

"You painted people into the picture with the mansion," she said aloud. Her body contorted into a pose on the divan. "Your servants and soldiers do not *work* for you—they are your slaves."

Yorch replied, untroubled, "As you will be."

He came to arrange her hair around her shoulders and the edge of the divan. He removed her arm from across her breast and tilted her chin so that she must look at him as he painted her.

He went to his large canvas, dipped his brush into a collection of jars on a platter, and began to paint Sajiana into the glamour of his mansion. Yorch painted with oils, and Sajiana could not deny his skill. She might have escaped the watercolor, in time. She knew she would never break free of this painting. The brink would have left Paddiglum by now, and when Mangcansten sent another glamourer after it, the glamourer would bypass Paddiglum altogether. Yorch, with his guilty conscience, had assumed that Mangcansten had de-tected his illegitimate use of magic. Sajiana knew better. As evil as it was, Yorch's magic had a limited reach. She had not sensed it from her meanderings around Paddiglum.

"Now, now," chuckled Yorch. "Your tears won't show in the paint-ing, so it's no use crying."

Under the compulsion, she had to take him literally. She could no longer even cry as the minutes crawled her closer to her enslave-ment.

Absorbed in his painting, Yorch did not hear the door to the stu-dio open. Sajiana heard, but under an order to hold her pose, could not turn. She did not see who it was until the brink walked on soft feet into view.

His dark chestnut hair was still disheveled, his velvet cape-coat torn to expose a tattered white blouse and one muscled shoulder. He gripped his kora sword in his hand. The brink rested the wickedly heavy tip of his kora against Yorch's neck.

"Stand and fight," the brink ordered in the steely voice of one accustomed to command.

Then, as if he were indeed the son of a noble house rather than a foul creature of magic, the young man stepped back and allowed Yorch to stagger to his feet and exchange his paintbrush for the sword he had earlier set aside.

Seconds into the duel, it was obvious that the brink mastered his sword as the greatest painters of Mangcansten mastered their art. Yorch sweated and puffed, trying to move his fat body out of the way more than to fight back. Yet a knowing smirk twisted Yorch's lips. From the divan where she lay, silent and immobilized by Yorch's orders, Sajiana saw the cause for his confidence. Yorch's soldiers, enslaved by his will, stormed up the stair and burst into the room. Six men now pressed the brink. They hacked at him with fierce downward motions of their kora swords, but he dodged in and out, slashing and tearing with his own blade as he swept by them. They began to lose limbs. Here a hand. There a leg. It became clear that they might as easily have lost heads, except that the young warrior did not seem to want to take their lives. Terror crept into their faces, and Sajiana suspected they would have fled, but Yorch's compulsion forced them to keep coming, even when blood gushed out from their wrists or knees.

Meanwhile, another soldier had crept into the attic from outside, through the casement window. Sajiana strove to cry out, to warn the brink, in vain. The newcomer slashed his kora directly into the back of the brink's neck. The blow nearly severed his head from his body.

The brink turned around and knocked the soldier out the window. The brink's head lolled at a silly angle. This development did not distress or slow the brink, but it shocked Yorch long enough for him to forget to maintain his hold over his soldiers. They fled at once.

"You're a brink!" Yorch stammered. "Wait, please! Don't kill me. We can reach an accommodation, I'm sure of it! Besides, all the wealth of this house is a glamour. If you kill me, who will maintain it for you? I will paint you anything you want—anything!"

"I am not a brink," said the brink. "And I don't want your bribes, you vile dog!"

For emphasis, the brink beheaded Yorch.

The brink finally noticed the odd state of his own head. He yanked out the blade still lodged in it and adjusted his head back on his neck. His skin smoothed over the wound, restoring him to perfect health.

The brink stared at the bloody kora, then turned to Sajiana in panic. "How did I do that?"

"You're a brink."

"How did I survive that wound? It would have killed any man!"

"You're not a man, you're a brink."

"Stop saying that!" He waved his sword.

The death of Yorch had, unfortunately, not altered the magic that bound Sajiana and the other servants of the mansion to the painting. Yorch's last commands no longer held true, so she was able to sit up and try to hide her nakedness with her hair and her arms. Yet, her spirit remained knotted to the house through the painting. She would not be able to leave as long as the painting survived. Since she was in the painting, she could not destroy it herself. She itched to grab Yorch's kora where it had clattered to the floor, but although she expected her swordsmanship a little surpassed Yorch's, she knew it would not be up to par to defeat the brink. Even if a stab *would* have killed him, which it obviously wouldn't.

"Will you kill me too, brink?" she asked without much hope.

He sheathed his kora. "I can't," he said. "Even if I wanted to. You hold me hostage, even as Yorch held you. I came here because you summoned me."

"You were able to slip out of my other drawing easily enough."

"This one would not let me go. I tried."

Sajiana felt a brief, irrational surge of pride in her work. It passed quickly, as she recalled that she too, remained bound. And there was a simple way for the brink to destroy her and free himself without attacking her directly.

"If I burn this painting, it will destroy this mansion, including the picture you drew," he said, walking to the canvas. "And it will destroy everyone painted into it, including you. That will free me, won't it?"

She didn't answer, but that was answer enough.

"Couldn't you just promise not to hunt me any more? An exchange. I cut the knots on this painting. You cut the knots on the drawing you made of me."

She pushed away the temptation to lie. "I have a duty to Mangcansten."

His huge, moist eyes pleaded with her. "Am I really a brink? How can I be a creature painted into existence when I remember my whole life? Brinks do not grow from childhood to adulthood. They are always as they were first painted."

"You remember being a child?"

"Yes." A thought brought despair to his face. "Could all my memories be false?"

"No. If you were a brink, you would not remember anything before you were brought to life that had not been in your painting."

"Then... I *am* human."

"No. If you were a man, you would be dead. You said it yourself."

"Am I immortal?"

Sajiana thought she must be a fool to tell him his strength if he did not know it. Yet she found herself answering gently, "No. But you cannot be killed by a man or by a woman, by a manmade object or an unmade object, inside or outside, on the land or on the sea, during the day or during the night. Only a glamourer can destroy you."

He absorbed that.

"Tell me what you remember," she prompted. "Was there anything... uhm, unusual about your family?"

"You might say so." He measured his trust of her, and must have found it small. Perhaps he deemed her no better than Yorch. "For many years, my parents could not have children. My mother said that she was...fortunate...that she finally had me."

"Did your mother paint?"

His pained silence answered her.

Sajiana whistled through her teeth. "No wonder you remember your childhood. Did you..." —it was a ridiculous question to ask a brink, "do you have a name?"

"Drajorian."

She raised her brows. "Your parents were bold to name a brink after the heir to the throne of Cammar."

"Apparently my parents were bold in ways I never imagined," he said dryly. "I knew my mother could be a stubborn woman. But this....You must understand, I was not raised in an isolated hamlet. I grew up surrounded by luminaries. None of them could have suspected, or there would have been consequences years ago."

She wondered how a powerful brink could have gone undetected so long. And what had changed so that suddenly Mangcansten had noticed him? "She must have first painted you as a baby."

"But then wouldn't I have remained a baby?"

"Not if she kept changing the portrait." She glanced over at the large painting that Yorch must have begun more than twenty years ago, that he had been touching up even now. "Year by year... maybe even day by day..."

He bowed his head. "So it is true. I am a monster."

There wasn't much Sajiana could say to that.

All at once, a yowl of despair issued from his throat. He raced to the painting, his hatchet-like kora sword raised over his head. Sajiana braced herself. She wondered if it would feel as though her flesh were being cut if he slashed the painting to shreds.

Instead, she felt a burden lift from her.

He had cut the knots.

The twenty-year old knots drifted away from the painting. From all over the mansion, the glad cries of servants and soldiers burst out. Then the mansion dissolved. Sajiana and the brink and two dozen or so others stood in the middle of a weed-strewn field. Here and there, real objects and pieces of furniture that had not been part of the glamour poked out of the grass. Sajiana recognized her rucksack and ran to it. She pulled on her traveling clothes with a deep sense of relief.

The brink followed her. He recovered her portfolio. The brink pulled out the drawing she had done of him and handed it to her, knot and all.

"Finish your job," he said. "Burn it."

The wind ruffled his hair. He stared at her with those limpid, haunted eyes.

Sajiana took the paper. It trembled in her fingers.

"If I untie the knots," she said, "They'll sense it. They can sense a brink from across the earth. They'll just send someone else after you."

"Burn it."

"I can't."

"I'd rather it be now. I'd rather it be you."

"I can't." She picked up her portfolio and put the drawing, still knotted, into her satchel. "If I don't burn it, but don't untie it, they won't sense you. I won't tug on your will. I won't summon you. You won't even know I still have your portrait."

He stared at her, full of questions.

"Go," she said. "Be free. It's a command."

Long after the brink had gone, and after Sajiana resumed her return trek across the moor to Mangcansten, she took the portrait out again. She studied the tousled hair and large eyes, the shadows on the face, the play of lights across the shoulders, the stance. She did not summon. She did not call. After a time, she sighed, and put the portrait away. She didn't knot a glamour cottage that night. She wanted to sleep under the stars.

Comments on

"Drawn to the Brink"

This is another story from *The Painted World* universe. It's an independent story, but also a loose sequel to, "Portrait of a Pretender." It first appeared in *WomanScapes*, an anthology published by DLSIJ Press.

I do a bit of oil painting, though not enough to acquire a true knack for it. For a while, I did paint every day, which I enjoyed. My painting also improved. I even opened a store on eBay and sold whimsical pictures of mermaids and big-eyed girls. This was shortly after I married and had my first child. I was desperate to "monetize" my creative efforts as an excuse to keep at them. I was still writing. That wasn't bringing in a lot of money, although I did sell two category romance novels to an ebook publisher, which, altogether, earned me about six thousand dollars in the first couple months and then a trickle of royalties. My husband was working two jobs to pay our mortgage, and I was earning just a few hundred dollars a month. It wasn't fair to him.

When I went back to grad school, I had to put the painting aside. If I had a dozen clones of myself, I think one would become a painter, but as it is, I decided to focus on writing. I enjoyed one art as a hobby, but (still) hoped to make the other a career. So if I couldn't paint (professionally), at least I could write about painting.

Originally *The Painted World* stories were intended to be part of a novel. However, I was having no luck selling my fantasy novels at this point. My romance novels were ebooks and didn't seem to count for much in the eyes of traditional publishing. I attended conventions, even one in New York, hosted by Backspace, where I met agents and had a number of requests for partials and fulls of Book One of *The Windwheel and the Maze*. I was hopeful one of those encounters would win me an offer of representation and a publishing contract with a Big House. Agents, editors and other writers gave me conflicting advice. Some said I should start on another novel right away. Others said I should try short stories to become known. I didn't want to invest another five or ten years perfecting a grand epic, only to start banging my head against the query wall again. There had to be a better way, I figured, some way I could publish as I went, without year+ intervals between production and publication.

I hoped that short story sales would gain me some credits in the genre of science fiction and fantasy. This was typically the route that aspiring sf&f writers took, right? Publish in fanzines, then little magazines, then prestigious magazines and anthologies. The trouble is, I'm not much of a short story writer, so I tried to cheat by breaking up a novel idea into its component parts. I dealt separately with the plots at the palace and the adventures of two glamourers, Sajiana and her rival from another Lodge, Fioma, out on the wild moors. I took for my inspiration the sword and sorcery short stories of Mercedes Lackey, featuring Tarma & Kethry.

To a certain extent, this worked. Many of the stories in this anthology appeared here and there over the years. In another sense, my plan was another flop. None of my short story credits amounted to much. The publications weren't grandiose enough for me to brag about in query letters, and even my friends often couldn't track down the stories after they faded from the front page.

Before this story found its original home in *WomanScapes*, it was turned down by a few editors who didn't like the open ending. I was reluctant to change it because I knew Sajiana and Drajorian would meet again. In fact, I have elaborate plans for the further adventures of Sajiana and Drajorian and Fioma and Othmodian and Lyadra. King Arnthom's death is yet to be avenged, and there are evil forces stirring in Cammar, things even worse than brinks.

GRACE

I heard a story once, and I should caution that I don't know if it's true. If it were about a dream come true, I would have reason to doubt it, but it is rather about disappointment come true, so I find it believable.

A woman born in a Central American country in the midst of a civil war fled from the violence as a child. Her name, shall we say, was Grace. She was terrified that she would die, but one night she had a dream, in which an angelic figure, or maybe a woman who looked like her dead grandmother, or maybe the Virgin Mary—I don't remember, and maybe she herself didn't either, by the time she shared the story—told her, "You will not die because you are going to achieve a Great Thing in your life, and God will keep you alive."

Grace was greatly cheered, not only by the knowledge that she was going to live, but that she would live with purpose, with an important destiny. As a child, she never told anyone her dream, but she cherished it in her heart, and thought back on it often. At first, the fact she and her family were able to make it into the United States seemed to confirm her dream, as did her excellent progress learning English, her good grades in high school and then college.

Yet decades slipped by, and though she married satisfactorily, and bore children she loved, she could not help but notice the dreary ordinariness of her life, the extremely non-special destiny that now seemed her lot, with no great, heaven-blessed achievement in sight. She aged and fattened and grayed, and by the time she pressed fifty, she felt worn out, worn down, disillusioned and despairing.

It was at this point that Grace finally shared her dream with a group of women who met with a psychologist for depression. The other women suggested to her that perhaps she had overlooked the obvious: perhaps God had kept her alive precisely to live and love, that in His eyes this was a Great Thing, maybe the Greatest thing. And if this were a story of a dream come true, or a Hallmark movie, Grace would have agreed and felt renewed gratitude and love for her family.

I warned you, however, that it was a story of a disappointment come true. The woman pretended to agree with the group, but in her heart, she was not comforted. She didn't want to be "special" in an ordinary way, treasured, like the sparrow, by God alone, she wanted to be special in the extraordinary way, recognized by thousands, or better still, hundreds of thousands of other human beings. She wanted to be famous, successful and important. That was how she had understood God's promise to her as a child; that was the dream that had sustained her. And though she recognized now, as an adult, that she had no right to expect to be important, certainly no right to demand it from destiny, still, she rebelled. She acknowledged, privately, the folly of her hubris, but this only deepened her bitterness.

God had lied to her.

When I heard this story, I was angry at the woman for her refusal to be comforted. Because, if she had been comforted by the women's interpretation of her dream, I felt, the story would have had a happy ending after all. She would have found grace where she least expected it. And yet, I was also aware that I was a hypocrite. Because, although I had never escaped a civil war, or been promised anything by an angel in a dream, nonetheless, as a child I had cherished the exact same hope, and as an adult, I awakened to the same disappointment.

Comments on

"Grace"

I can't sustain gloom for the length of a novel. I love happy endings. But my short stories frequently end in tragedy or at least melancholy. When I am depressed, my response is to write a story, the bleaker the better. For unknown reasons, that revives my spirits.

This story is not really fiction. I did know a woman who had a dream, and one day, when I had received my third reject letter in one week, I wrote this story about her, but really about myself. I think all artists are secretly egomaniacs, and I'm hardly special in that respect. Despite the constant temptation to grandiosity, I tried to keep my expectations modest. I wanted to write for a living—by which I mean earn a living wage—but I didn't expect to get rich from it.

By the time I wrote *Grace*, ten years had passed from the time I'd run away from home to be a writer. I'd traveled around the world, found a cyborg to marry, spawned a few hellbeasts, er, children, and decided to return to school.

I gave in to the voice of reason and common sense, and worked to become a college professor. At first, I tried to write fiction while going to school, but gradually, work overwhelmed me or drained me. I sent out queries, and these were rejected at various stages. If I received a rejection after sending out a partial or a full, this was a cause for celebration—a better class of failure. I reached the "full" stage more often now, but I was running out of agents to spam. I spent as much time crafting query letters as I did writing new material. I obsessed over revisions. I become depressed and self-doubting. I promised myself I would write as soon as I had time. But as babies appeared and as financial burdens increased, I had less and less time, and I felt more and more guilty for not bringing in a sustainable income. Years went by, and I constantly fiddled with my novel, or dashed out morbid short stories. I seemed to have fallen into a rut.

I had been working on my epic *The Windwheel and the Maze* for an entire decade. (In related news, although 2000-2010 was supposed to a bring a manned space voyage to Jupiter to witness it turning into a star, reality had turned out to be a cancelled space program. Reality was really letting me down.) I read agents' blogs and editors' blogs, and they universally agreed that if you shopped your novel that long, you were a lunatic who ought to get over yourself already and write something new. This depressed me tremendously, and instead of heeding the advice, I kept researching new bits for my novel. I told myself to give up the idea of writing as a career. Yet I couldn't let go. I had become so obsessed with learning the publishing side of the business, I sometimes forgot why I was writing at all. At times, I hated it. I definitely hated my novel. It was the worst dreck in the universe. Why *would* anyone want to read it?

Writing, just like theater, is a performance. It's a just a dress rehearsal until you put it before an audience. I was in a bind because I couldn't let it go until I could let it play. But no one would let me on stage.

Then came the worst blow. I was told that I was not a fit match for my graduate program. My interests were "too broad" for a PhD candidate. When I received this news, I was a week away from giving birth to my third son, a child we could not afford. The economy had done a swan dive, we owed more on our house than it was worth, and our outgo was exceeding our income every month. At this point, I had failed at everything. I failed at my childhood dream of being a novelist and I failed at my adult dream of being an academic. I had failed myself, and I failed my family. Suicide offered a romantic way out, but was neither practical nor fair. It was just another form of running away, and running away was no longer an option.

TOMORROW WE DANCE

1. *Vexation*

THE BONE WHISTLER'S NAME EVOKES nothing but terror and revulsion now, so it is hard to explain to those who had not yet been born what he meant to us back then.

As a child of five, six, seven years old, I herded aurochsen for our family. When my brother Vumo was old enough, he helped me. We lived in a three-room adobe house in the tribehold on top of a mesa in a large desert valley cut by a river. We knew we lived at the center of the world; we knew our tribe was the most important in the world. On festival days, my father and mother, and my mother's sister and her husband, and all my siblings and cousins, joined the crowds in the central plaza of the tribehold to watch the Tavaedi dancers. To the beat of drums and the whistle of flutes, they danced magic. Each Tavaedi wore the mask and elaborate costume dyed in one of the six Chroma, and even back then, before I knew I had magic, I could see the ribbons of colored light they wove as they danced. Most people could not.

I was there the day of the celebration of our final victory over the faery Aelfae. We had fought them for millennia, and finally, invited the last of them to a feast to make peace. It was a trick. When our clever War Chief gave the signal, our Tavaedies and Zavaedies, who are also warriors, rose up, and slaughtered all of the Aelfae, the last of their kind. Their bodies turned to dust.

And on this day, we all celebrated.

Our War Chief, who danced the rain, and our Vaedi, who danced the rainbow, performed the victory *tama* to bless our animals, crops and tribe. They danced together as gracefully as two eagles soared in the sky. He caught her by the waist and spun and twirled her, and then, toward the end of the dance, the culmination of the *tama* that would bless us, a flute hit the wrong note, he threw her into the air...

...and did not catch her.

She fell on the adobe stage, and her head twisted backwards against her neck. Her blood made a dark mark on the white clay.

We boys were among the first to notice when our aurochsen began to sicken. At first, it did not seem too bad, just a dry, husky cough. It worsened, however. Soon the aurochsen began to cough pinkish spittle—speckles of blood. Within a few weeks, their whole bodies would shake and heave each time they coughed out huge clots of blood and phlegm.

They suffered diarrhea and could no longer eat. Toward the end, they looked more like skeletons than living beasts. Their eyes rolled up from the agony of their suffering, their muzzles frothed with saliva, and after weeks more of this agony, they died. The meat of such beasts was inedible—it was as though they had rotted from the inside out.

Nor were our aurochsen the only ones to suffer. Anyone whose aurochs began to cough immediately traded it away for a healthy beast, or even for goats or peccaries, and as the diseased aurochsen spread through trade and travel, so too did the blood-cough.

We plied the Tavaedies with gifts, and asked them to dance a cure to save our herds. But though they took our gifts, they could not cure our aurochsen.

Only a new Vaedi could cleanse the blood that had been spilled. Otherwise, the old Vaedi's blood would continue to cry for vengeance through the lives of our cattle. But there were no more girls who danced all six Chromas, and the Tavaedi secret societies could not agree on which of their dancers deserved to be the new Vaedi.

In the meantime, we did what we could to salvage our herds. For the matriarchs of the tribehold decreed that the only way to stop the hex from spreading was to sacrifice all the cattle in any infected herd.

My parents split up our herd into thirds and sent them to different pastures. I watched one herd, my brother Vumo another, and my sister, Gia and cousin Loola, the final herd. In my herd and my sister's, a few of the aurochsen began to cough, and soon to cough blood. Vumo's herd stayed clean. My father said we must kill the two herds that were infected, every head, to protect the one good herd. I loved those beasts and cried when I heard the decree.

My mother's younger sister and her husband and their two daughters also lived with us, and their aurochsen grazed with ours. My uncle did not want his aurochsen killed. He was sure that those who weren't coughing could be saved. So he ordered his daughters, Loola and Herba, to secretly move the healthy aurochsen from the condemned herds into the healthy herd. My sister Gia found out and told Vumo and me, so all we children knew about my uncle's scheme. Still, we stuck together and helped him move the cattle in the night.

My uncle acted from his greed on his own behalf, and we from our generosity on the poor beasts' behalf, but both greed and generosity had the same effect. The aurochsen we thought clean had been infected, and no sooner moved, began to cough. We killed them, but too late. They had brought the blood-cough to the herd that had been clean. If we had done as my father ordered, we might have kept a third of our original herd alive. As it was, we lost all but nine cows, out of a hundred.

All across the Rainbow Labyrinth tribehold, other clans suffered similarly. Some saved as many as half of their herds, but few more than that. And as clans took their herds and fled the tribehold for clanholds in the hinterland, the hex spread ever outward, until there was no clan in the whole tribe who did not fear the blood-cough. Clanholds began to shoot arrows at any visitors who traveled with aurochsen.

To add to our misery, the dead cattle, whose corpses, remember, could not be eaten, were often left out on the hills to rot. An army of rats rose to gnaw on the bones left by the larger predators. Many of these rats also began to destroy the crops in the fields, so now, having lost our meat and milk, we were also in danger of losing our bread and beans.

And still, the Tavaedies could not decide on a Vaedi! In their secret underground rooms, they bickered and dithered, and sought their own advancement, while we ordinary people desperately needed strong leadership.

Then he arrived.

The Bone Whistler.

2. *Eradication*

WHEN THE BONE WHISTLER first arrived at the tribehold, he was greeted with neither acclaim nor scorn, for he was just another vagabond from the countryside. As the blood-cough spread throughout the land, many such scraggly types fled to the tribehold, expecting us to have the magic to solve their problems. They were disillusioned to know that we were the source of their troubles, not the solution.

The Bone Whistler soon proved different. He was young in those days, handsome, according to the women folk, and undeniably charming. He wore the attire and title of a Zavaedi, although he never said with whom he had studied or which clan he called home. Since he wore all white, even then, no one ever knew what Chroma he danced. When asked by other Tavaedies what his Chroma was, he told them he danced "Sulula," but, he added, only the most powerful dancers could perceive such a subtle hue. Most people laughed at this nonsense, but others were baffled. Sulula? Did he mean Red or Blue or Green? Did he have six Chromas, or three or one? His detractors said he had no colors at all.

He spoke with a strange accent; some said he wasn't even of our tribe. He had no wife, but he did have a little daughter, just eight or nine she must have been, when he first arrived. Unlike her jolly father, she never smiled, but in those days, we seldom saw her.

He had his bone flute from the first. However, either it did not yet have the power it later had, or he chose not to show the reach of his ambition so early. In either case, he used the flute only to play and dance in the back alleys of the tribehold, the narrow passages between blocks of adobe houses, where midden piles churned the orange clay ground to reeking mud. Rats crawled over the filth, fighting beggars for the scraps thrown from the rooftops of the better-off, yet his cape was always clean, bright white.

He was kind and humble. He had a sense of humor. Above all, he feared nothing. In that time of great fear, people drew close to him to bask in his fearlessness. And he encouraged them. If there were destitute people who could not afford to give gifts to the Tavaedies, he agreed to dance magic for them for whatever scrap they could give. The poor people of the tribehold loved him for this, and to the same extent as their love, the Tavaedies hated him.

I was there when they finally confronted him. A crowd gathered when we saw the Zavaedies and Tavaedies, fully masked and armed, marching through the streets. We knew they must be going to confront the Bone Whistler. We children pushed to the front of that crowd, so I saw and heard everything.

"Strange Zavaedi," said the old Rain Dancer, husband to the Vaedi who had died. He seemed tired and afraid. It was said he had not danced since his wife's death. He was the one who had dropped her, and though it was an accident, many blamed him. Maybe he blamed himself. He looked shriveled and sounded shrew. "Your mother's clan is not known to us, nor did any of our societies give you leave to dance magic here."

The Bone Whistler smiled. His eyes twinkled. Yet he answered politely. "Zavaedies, do not be angry at me for helping those you have already refused."

The crowd loved his audacity. We laughed and cheered.

The Rain Dancer's neck flushed red under his wooden mask. "You must leave at once."

"By whose order?" asked the Bone Whistler. He raised his arms to beseech the people. "Is this your will? Do you want me to leave at once?"

"No!" cried many voices from the crowd.

My brother Vumo and I exchanged a look.

"Can they make him leave?" asked Vumo.

"I don't know," I said. Anger swelled in me at the injustice.

"These people have no say," said the Rain Dancer, gesturing at all of us, the common people. "It is a matter for the secret societies to decide."

"That's not fair!" shouted Vumo, along with many other boos and catcalls.

"No, no, it's quite alright," said the Bone Whistler, still smiling. "I understand the Rain Dancer's fear. What proof do you have that I am a Zavaedi, that I have earned my Shining Name?"

"That was not—" began the Rain Dancer, but the Bone Whistler kept going.

"I will prove it, with a simple *tama*. I will rid the whole tribehold and surrounding valley of the plague of rats." He beamed at the Rain Dancer and the armed Tavaedies behind him. "Surely then you must agree that I am who I say I am."

My brother and I and the other children began to jump up and down with excitement, for we were the main ones who had to fight off the rats with sticks and slings. The adults took their cues from us. "Yes! Yes! Rid us of the rats!"

The Rain Dancer pursed his lips on sour defeat. He could not refuse to let the Bone Whistler try a spell that the Tavaedies had not been able to do. He conferred with the masked men and women behind them. When he turned back to the Bone Whistler, he sounded sly.

"We don't wish to let you try such a difficult spell by yourself. What if you make matters worse?"

"You lot aren't doing it!" cried the crowd, and, "Give him his chance!" and "Yes, let him prove it!"

"Very well, let it be noted that we warned you," said the Rain Dancer. "We were planning to do it ourselves—"

The crowd shouted out in derision.

"And no one will be happier if you succeed," continued the Rain Dancer. "But, in view of the risk, there must be some penalty if you fail. If you are as great a Zavaedi as you claim, then you will be willing to accept our terms, which are these: If even so much as a single rat remains after you perform your spell, you must concede failure, and you must leave our tribehold."

The fickle crowd agreed with this judgment too, and the Rain Dancer raised his arms to accept their hollers of accord.

"I will give you a day to decide," he told the Bone Whistler smugly, apparently in the hope that the upstart would sneak out in the middle of the night like a coward.

"I don't need a day, or even an hour," the Bone Whistler said, as unafraid as he had always been. "I will do it now."

The crowd cheered.

Then and there, he lifted the bone flute to his lips. He played and danced. Never had I heard a note so true, so pure. Everyone stilled to give homage to the haunting music. Even we boys stopped our heckling and roughhousing in a shock of transported emotion.

I was concentrating so hard on the flute song that I can't remember when I first noticed the squeaks and skittering. It wasn't until I felt something furry scrape my ankle that I saw the rats. I yowled and hit one with a stick. But more came.

Screams curdled the multitude. Individuals peeled away from the crowd, fleeing the oncoming streams of rats.

The rats looked as though they might attack the Bone Whistler, so eagerly did they run toward him from all directions. They climbed down adobe walls, scaled up out of stone wells, jumped from gourds and baskets hanging from balconies, and scrambled out of piles of rubbish between houses. Yet, just when they reached him, they paused, sat back on their haunches, and stared up at him. Soon they encircled him, pressed as closely as they could to one another, yet leaving him an arm's length of clearance in a circle all around. Their little brown heads tilted back to watch him, their whiskers bobbed with the music, as rapt an audience as one could ask.

The humans had to back away to make room for the rats. Most people's reaction wavered between admiration and horror. For me and the other young ones, however, there was no hesitation. The Bone Whistler had just become our most cherished hero.

He winked at me. At me!

"Did you see that? Was he looking at us?" Vumo asked me excitedly.

The Bone Whistler skipped away, still dancing and playing his flute. The rats made way for him, and they followed him.

All through the streets of the tribehold he skipped and danced and played the bone flute, calling the rats to him. A group of boys,

Vumo and myself included, ran after the rats, though we had to stay farther and farther behind.

By the time the Bone Whistler skipped out the front gate of the tribehold, we could only see a tiny silhouette at the head of a seething mass of fur and tails.

We stood at the edge of the mesa outside the tribehold wall, watching this tiny figure in white lead a swarm of rats, numerous as a herd of aurochsen, out across the valley floor all the way to the edge of the box canyon, where the river cut the rock.

The Bone Whistler stood alone on a high boulder over the river. We could no longer hear the music of the flute, but we could see the impact his dance and song had upon the rats. In wave after wave, they threw themselves over the edge of the rocks, into the white water.

The sun set, and the rats kept coming. Moonglow saw more waves of suicidal rats, a flood that slowed to a stream and finally to a trickle of stragglers. The mighty river patiently bore away the corpses all day and all night. Dawn found the river clean and sparkling and every last rat gone.

Vumo and I told our families about the miracle magic of the Bone Whistler. Other children must have done the same. All the tribehold prepared to greet him as if he were a victor in a war—which, in a way, he was. The secret societies must have realized that they could not turn him out now. They tried to co-opt the celebration instead. They provided a feast for all the people in the Grand Plaza. As usual, my brother and I squirmed in where we didn't belong, to watch our hero from underneath the dancer's platform.

In the middle of the feast, the Rain Maker stood up to give a speech.

"Bone Whistler, you promised that if even one rat remained in the tribehold, you would concede defeat and quit our hold."

"I have driven every last rat into the river," said the Bone Whistler. "I kept my word and proved my power."

"I think not," said the Rain Maker. He threw something down. It raced down the center of the eating mat until it found a choice morsel to nibble. Several women screamed. "A rat! A rat!"

The Bone Whistler scowled. The geniality he had always shown before tore at the edges, hinting at a depth of fury and hatred I could barely comprehend.

"You withheld that rat deliberately." He stood up. He said, in a cold and terrible voice, "You will regret betraying me."

Then he turned to us, the common people.

"There is a great magic," he said. "Older than this world, stronger than death. I know you have lost cattle. But this magic can bring back the aurochsen. I know you have lost loved ones. But this magic can resurrect the dead."

"Blasphemy!" The Rain Maker pounded the feast mat. "No magic can do that! No Chroma is stronger than the call of the Black Lady!"

"No Chroma known to you," sneered the Bone Whistler. "But there is a color you have never heard of before, a color stronger than all the others. It is not Red or Blue, Yellow or Green, Purple or Orange. It is a new Chroma! The color of Sulula."

"Never has anyone heard such nonsense! There is no color called Sulula!"

"There is," said the Bone Whistler. "Only those pure of heart can see it. But there is a way to let *everyone* see Sulala, which will bring the dead back to life. And I know how! Whoever wants to see the secret color and resurrect the dead must follow me."

The Zavaedies and Tavaedies rocked back on their heels and laughed so hard they had to hold their jiggling bellies.

"Can you believe the gall of this fool?" they cried.

A small smile touched the Bone Whistler's handsome face. He lifted the bone flute to his lips and began to play.

At the sound of his music, all the young people began to dance. The youngest children joined in, first, then the older ones, including my brother Vumo and me. Finally, the Initiates, the young men and women at the dawn of their strength and beauty, danced too. The Bone Whistler lifted his flute in the air and shouted, "All who believe in Sulula, follow me!"

And before their eyes, the Zavaedies and Tavaedies and elder aunties and uncles watched their sons and daughters follow the Bone Whistler out of the tribehold.

3. *Resurrection*

THOSE WERE THE BEST DAYS of my life. The Bone Whistler set up a camp in the hills outside the tribehold. Young people flocked to the call of his flute, but soon we were joined by others.

In the earliest days of our tribehold, many generations ago, *all* Tavaedies had danced six Chromas. Each generation, fewer and fewer dancers of all six Chromas were born, but it was still true that the more Chromas a dancer had, the more respect he earned. By the time I was born, there were almost no six-banded dancers left, but it was still a requirement that to advance from Tavaedi to Zavaedi, you had to dance two or more Chromas – to be Many-Banded, an Imorvae. The Morvae, dancers with just one Chroma, were made to feel inferior because of their supposed deficiency. They resented the restrictions against them, but they were powerless to change the rules.

The Bone Whistler changed all that. He not only welcomed the Morvae, he favored and flattered them. They were not inferior to Imorvae, he said, but in fact quite superior! His own daughter was a Morvae, and she had a marvelous ability, though he didn't tell us what it was. She had just passed her Initiation. That was Nangi, of course, and we would learn to our sorrow her power soon enough. All that mattered then was that if the Bone Whistler's own daughter was a Morvae, it must be a matter of pride, not shame.

Morvae Tavaedies began to join our herd. Not just Initiates, either, as at first, but elders with great power. These, the Bone Whistler elevated to Zavaedies, earning their fierce devotion. I was twelve, my brother Vumo was eleven, and we could not wait for our Initiation. We already suspected we both had magic, for we could see the fae. We hoped we would both prove to be Morvae, which showed how much things had changed in just a few years.

The split between the Morvae and Imorvae had not yet grown to an unbridgeable gulf. On the contrary, in those days, it seemed all divisions between humanity were of little lasting import. The Bone Whistler attracted Imorvae followers too, not to mention droves of common people, for what he promised benefited all mortal kind.

He offered us eternity – immortality for the generation living, and the resurrection of the dead.

Resurrection! All our loved ones and ancestors would walk the earth again!

Immortality! We would dwell with them forever.

Free of death, free of sorrow, a thousand years of gold tomorrow, all this would come to pass and more, the blind would see, the mute would sing, no drought would sting, no flood would pour. In amazing hue each thing would glow as none had ever seen before. Sulula, the color no one had seen, would make all things new and strange, would conquer Death and grief and pain.

When our eyes were opened, when the Resurrection came, we would all see magic, we would all earn a Shining Name. We would all dance colors -- all the Six and Sulula too. No more would some have and others not. No more would some inherit greatness like the sky, the others only dirt and rot. We would all have wings.

Our faith was proved by astonishing events. Miracles happened. Dancers besides the Bone Whistler began to see Sulula, and then to dance this marvelous new Chroma. It was most common in new Initiates, but some of the Zavaedies the Bone Whistler had chosen discovered they could now see and dance Sulula, who never had before. Whenever a new Sulula Tavaedi arose, the crowds would go with him or her to the Bone Whistler, who would confirm, "Yes! I see Sulula in your aura!"

I could never see anything in their auras, but I was not yet an Initiate, and often could not read auras well, so I didn't worry. I was sure my power would come in time.

One day, Vumo and I were in the crowd when a beautiful young woman stood up and walked to the stage in front of the Bone Whistler. She was utterly, starkly, ravishingly naked. We, and every male in the herd, watched her in shock and joy as she began to dance, absolutely nude. We laughed and clapped and thought her mad.

Her uncle, though himself a follower of the Bone Whistler, was not so happy at her display.

"What are you doing, toad-headed girl? You are humiliating yourself and me! Why are you dancing without a mask or a scrap of clothing?"

"Oh, uncle!" She laughed, quite sure of herself, "You cannot see, but I *am* wearing mask and dress, all of shining Sulula, and I am dancing Sulula too!"

We stopped our mocking, uncertain then. She looked naked to us, but only the most powerful Zavaedies could see Sulula. Everyone looked to the Bone Whistler.

He studied her while she danced.

"O my people!" he cried. "I have never seen a stronger dancer of Sulala! She is a gift indeed to us all! What is your name, great Lady?"

Her uncle hurried forward. "I am Sambolo! She is *my* niece, Gladola!"

"Congratulations!" said the Bone Whistler. "She is destined to be the new Vaedi! Her aura of Sulula shines so brightly I suspect even those who have never seen it before must surely see the glow! Dance, Vaedi, dance, that even the weakest among us may witness and believe!"

Gladola began to dance again. I still saw no light about her, none at all. I cursed my own lack of magic.

Someone in the crowd leapt to his feet. "I am not a Tavaedi, but I *see* it! I see Sulula!"

"I *am* a Tavaedi, and I see it too!" exclaimed another voice from the crowd.

"I see her dress too—how beautiful it is!"

"I see it too!"

"I see Sulula!"

Soon people all around us jumped up to testify they could see Gladola's aura of Sulula, her dress of Sulula, her crown of Sulula, her blinding Pattern of Sulula light.

Beside me, Vumo squinted and squirmed. Then happiness lit his face. He pointed. "I think I see it too, Vio! Can you see it? Can you see Sulula?"

I stared at her with all my might. The sun shone on her naked breasts and thighs, glinting off the sweat sheened skin. I had never seen anything so beautiful in my whole life. Maybe she was beautiful because she shimmered with the light of Sulula. So maybe... maybe I could see it! I told myself I could, and as soon as I was sure I had seen it once, I didn't worry whether it flickered in and out, making it difficult for me to catch sight of it again.

"Yes!" I shouted. "I see it! I see Sulula!"

"So do I!" said Vumo. We both jumped up and down with the rest, screaming, "I see it! I see Sulula!"

❑ ❑ ❑

You may ask. Did I really see Sulula?

In later years, I asked myself that question many times.

I saw hope. I saw my friends. I saw my brother. I saw the future. I saw eternity. I saw a world without war, without disease, without cruelty. I saw peace and light and beauty and love, triumphant, unending and untainted. I saw, I believed. And for me, because my faith was the color of Sulula. I saw Sulula.

4. *Prognostication*

EVERYONE WANTED TO KNOW. How would we bring about the new day? When would Sulula shine over everything, making all the world new, giving us the wings of immortality and resurrecting our dead? We all looked to the Bone Whistler for answers, but it was always Gladola or her uncle Sambolo who answered questions about the prophecy. We did not differentiate at the time, for the Bone Whistler always stood behind them, supporting them with tunes on his flute, but we were to be reminded of it later.

"To bring about the New Day, you must cleanse yourself of the old," announced Gladola. "You must kill every head of cattle, every horse in your kraal, every goat and every bird. You must burn your fields clean of every crop. Then build for yourselves new kraals and new granaries, to hold the overflowing bounty that will come to you. For on the New Day, Sulula–colored aurochsen and Sulula-hued horses will appear and the granaries will overflow with Sulula corn and beans. No more shall we have to labor for our food, all will come to us of its own. But only those who show their faith will be rewarded with the bounty. Those who are blind to Sulula will be unable to find or eat the new things."

Vumo and I had brought our aunt and uncle into the flock, along with our sister and cousin. Our father, however, had been suspicious of the Bone Whistler from the start, and when he heard the prophecy he declared the man was either a damn fool or a charlatan. When we defended the Bone Whistler, our father shouted at us. He chased us at spear point from our mother's house and ordered us never to return.

We moved permanently into the Bone Whistler's camp, where we had spent most of our time before anyway.

We attended rallies of the Bone Whistler. These were often led these days by Sambolo, the uncle of the presumptive Vaedi, Gladola.

"I see Sulula!" he shouted. "What do you see?"

"We see Sulula!" the crowd roared.

"What do you see?"

"We see Sulula!"

"What do you see?"

"We see Sulula!"

We shouted. We danced. Potters and tanners and herders danced, unashamed, unmasked, shoulder to shoulder with Tavaedies and Zavaedies. Morvae were the equal of Imorvae. We were all sisters and brothers. We all shared a single Chroma. We all danced Sulula. We danced the new, the ultimate taboo. We danced a new world into being.

And piercing the roar of the crowd, we could always hear the haunting melody of the flute of the Bone Whistler.

The more people joined the flock, the more the old Rain Maker and the Zavaedies still loyal to him feared and hated the Bone Whistler. They wanted to stop us. The elders of the tribehold also loathed the Bone Whistler, who had turned their own children against them. They urged the Rain Maker to do something.

He invited the Bone Whistler to return to the tribehold to talk, but the Bone Whistler refused.

"If you want to talk to me, come out here, into my camp, and talk," the Bone Whistler replied through a messenger.

Of course, at first, the Rain Maker responded in fury to this insult. But what could he do? There was still no acknowledged Vaedi in the tribehold, and he lost followers by the day.

I was there, in the first several rows of witnesses, at the historic meeting when the Rain Maker finally agreed to come out to the Bone Whistler's camp. A sept of his Zavaedies came with him. They wanted the Rain Maker to say once and for all whether the color Sulula existed or not. We, on the other hand, wanted the Rain Maker to acknowledge Gladola as the Vaedi, and step down to let the Bone Whistler be her new War Chief.

The Bone Whistler held a feast for his visitors. Many of his most loyal followers were invited, including children such as Vumo and me, who had been with him from the start. But if we expected the Bone Whistler to repay the rudeness the Zavaedies had shown him, we underestimated him. The Bone Whistler proved the most gracious of hosts. After plying with his guests drink and victuals, he addressed the Rain Maker by name, as an equal.

"Thank you for coming, Wuko. I know it was not an easy decision." He smiled gently. "I don't know if you realize this, but I knew your wife, Nyala. She deserved her reputation as the most beautiful human woman in all of Faearth. Even a fae lord would have been hard-pressed to resist her. I truly sorrowed when I heard of her tragic death." The Rain Maker, Wuko, frowned, but the Bone Whistler went on smoothly, "How glad you must be to know you will see her again soon."

"You know very well she is dead." Wuko scowled.

"And the dead shall soon rise from their graves and be again as we knew them."

"So *you* say."

"So I say. Ah, how you must be looking forward to holding her again. When the crowd of resurrected ancestors come thronging to find their loved ones, you will know her, I imagine, by the river otter fur she always used to wear on the trim of her dress. How will you greet her when she rushes into your arms? Have you thought of what you want to say to her first? Or will you simply lift her into the air and swing her for joy? For you yourself will be changed too. Your back won't pain you as it does now, those winter white hairs will be summer brown again. And who will you greet next? Your mother or your father? Or the son you lost during the war with the Aelfae?"

Wuko could find no answer, but the Bone Whistler anticipated none.

He lifted his flute and played for the visitors.

Gladola danced, stark naked, as always. We were used to it by now, but the Zavaedies stared.

When she finished her dance, one of the Zavaedies laughed. "Fa! She is a fraud! She has no magic. Not a single Chroma. Tell them, Rain Maker. There is no such color as this so-called 'Sulula.' There can never be a *new* color. Denounce the sham!"

Wuko wrinkled his brow. His eyes darted hither and about, like restless birds perched on the cliff of his prominent nose.

"There are many more colors than those we give name to," he said slowly. "There are many shades, many tints and tones. Maybe there are colors no human has ever seen before." His wing-like eyelashes fluttered in rheumy doubt. "But." He coughed apologetically. "But where in the rainbow is this new color, this Sulula, found? Is it to the far side of Red or does it hide on the other side of Purple? Is it between Orange and Yellow or between Green and Blue? No one can seem to agree. I hear arguments from all sides. When no-one can agree on what this Sulula is, or where to place it, or what things in nature are colored this color, it is hard, very hard..." He pinched his lips. His gaze took flight to a far horizon, deliberately fleeing the eyes of anyone in the assembly. "But I cannot say it doesn't exist. I have never seen it myself. How can I say what others have seen? I have seen things and colors no-one else has seen, how can I say what others have seen?"

"But, Rain Maker," his companion insisted, gritting his teeth at this betrayal, "Why is it only now that humans can see this supposed new color? Isn't it more likely that this man is lying, leading people to pretend to see something which isn't there at all?"

"How can I say what others have seen?" repeated Wuko. "How can you?"

Sambolo leaned forward. "Then you will accept my niece as Vaedi?"

Wuko would not go so far. "The Vaedi must have Six Chromas. She must be able to dance the Rainbow. That is our oldest law.

Whether this girl dances Sulula or not, whether Sulula is a real color or not, it is not the rainbow. This girl cannot be Vaedi."

So nothing was decided and neither side left satisfied. However, in the aftermath of the meeting a strange thing happened. Though Wuko had actually said he'd been unable to see Sulula, in Gladola's dance or anywhere at all, because he also had refused to say it could not exist, rumors became confused as they spread. First, people were excited because he had not denounced Sulula, which in the telling became that he had seen it himself, which in further telling became that he had indeed endorsed Gladola as Vaedi, but his own Zavaedies would not let him bring her back to the tribehold. Because of this, many people who remained loyal to the Rain Maker, and even more of those who had been wavering, now took the Bone Whistler's prophecy seriously.

More and more people took the pledge to bring about the new day. We knew the price of the resurrection would be to sacrifice the things of the present day. We prepared to slaughter our herds and burn our crops.

5. Anticipation

THE PROPHECY OF THE BONE WHISTLER had spread far, past the tribehold, to clan-klatches and clanholds across the tribal lands of Rainbow Labyrinth, even to neighboring tribes. Though Sambolo resisted naming a date, at last he said that the new day would dawn the first full moon after the Spring Equinox. *If*, he cautioned, if we had purified the land by then, the new day would dawn.

To purify the land, we must slaughter all our beasts and destroy our crops. Every family among us had some experience with this, for we had slaughtered aurochsen during the blood-cough plague, and burned crop seed ruined by rats. This was different, however, for this time, we were to hold nothing back. We were not trying to save a remnant, as before, but to destroy everything.

Manic merriment erupted. A prolonged festival of blood-letting began. People slaughtered their beasts in their yards, in kivas, in the road. These were good cattle, clean and safe, so they roasted the meat, and baked corn into loaves and cakes, and made delicious dishes of every sort. You could walk the length of the tribal lands of Rainbow Labyrinth and pause every hour on your way to feast with a different family.

This, I thought, must be a taste of how the new day would be. Before, because of the blood-cough plague, I had always gone a few bites short at every meal. My belly had never been really *full*. I was thirteen years old now. I had always lived with hunger—until now. For the first time, I had to drag my belly after me every time I rose from a meal.

And yet...

Everyone must have had secret doubts. Even I did, though, being young, my faith was stronger than most. These niggling fears only made us less tolerant of those who dared voice their doubts aloud, or worse, openly defied the prophecy.

My brother and I joined a gang of boys, one of many spontaneously formed, who roamed the countryside. We sat down at the feasts thrown by the believers and painted white skulls upon the houses of the doubters. At night, older boys, in bone masks and white war costumes would come to the marked houses, kill the hoarded aurochsen and take the seed from the granaries. Sometimes the doubters would give in and join us, dining on the feast before the flesh rotted. What else could they do?

They *could* fight back. Some did. This forced us to become more organized. We started spontaneously, as I said, but before long the Zavaedies loyal to the Bone Whistler organized our rabble into disciplined septs. All of these Zavaedies happened to be Morvae, though at this time, there were still Imorvae Tavaedies allied with us as well. Pitched battles became more common between the believers and the doubters.

Though I had not yet reached the age of Initiation, I wore white war paint and a skull mask. Both believers and doubters scrambled to please me when they saw me coming. I could walk into a stranger's house and demand a blanket, a basket, a beer, whatever I wanted, and it would be given to me with obsequious smiles. I learned to swagger. My stomach was full of meat, and my head was full of myself.

Then Vumo and I heard disturbing news. Our parents remained among the doubters. Another sept of boys had identified my father and tagged his house, but one of the boys knew he was our father and warned us. We had to set him straight.

Vumo and I went to my parent's house. We found my mother, father, and sister huddled inside, terrified, for they saw our skull masks and did not know us.

"It's me, father," I said, sliding the mask back up on my head.

My father responded by shouting insults at me. My mother and sister calmed him down, and forced him to sit still and listen to my plea.

"Father, I am not here to force you to do anything. I have not even come here to ask you to change your mind." I knelt before him. "I have come to beg you to change your heart. I have heard the prophecy from the Vaedi herself. I believe it. I beg you to believe it to. A better world is waiting for us, if we but have the courage to reach for it. We have to have faith. We cannot hold onto the soiled things of this day and the pure things of the new day at the same time. To catch the bounty about to be given us, we must let go of what we are now clutching so tightly."

"Boy, never have I heard such foolishness. How can I believe in something I can't see?"

"Father, do you remember when the blood-cough plague was spreading? You split our herd into three parts. When aurochsen in two of those showed signs of the blood-cough, you ordered us to kill all the beasts in those two parts. If we had listened, we would have saved a third of our herd. Instead, we tried to spare some of the aurochsen, because we could see no disease in them, and we didn't believe in what we couldn't see. We were wrong before, you are wrong now. I am asking you to believe. This whole world is diseased, but by letting go of it, we will save the best of all."

Tears came to my father's eyes. He clasped me to him. Much more was said that night, but all I remember is my fierce joy. I had changed his mind. I had saved him.

Meanwhile, to protect themselves from our attacks, other doubters began to disguise themselves as believers. During the day, they would travel to the clanhold with the Bone Whistler to attend our rallies.

"We see Sulula! We see Sulula!" they would shout, louder than the rest. Then, at night, they would go home and tend their secret gardens and sequester their herds in hidden fields high in the hills. We called them night-hoarders, those who tried to hoard food. They were ghastly, selfish people. They cared only about keeping themselves and their families alive, they didn't care their skepticism could destroy the new day for all of us.

We had an antidote for the poison of hypocrisy. The Bone Whistler's daughter, Nangi, had the uncanny ability to eat people's thoughts and tell the taste of their thinking. Even as an Initiate, she was terribly ugly. Her teeth were crooked, her face acne-scarred and she always hunched and scowled. Everyone pretended to like her, for her father's sake, but of course she knew everyone was lying. No one liked her.

We boys would finger people we suspected were night-hoarders. The warriors would kidnap them in the night and bring them before Nangi, who would read their thoughts. Usually, they were guilty, and Nangi would tell us where they were hiding their caches.

The hoarders themselves disappeared.

I didn't know what happened to them. I didn't allow myself to think about it. It didn't seem important, until my father had to go before Nangi and be tested. Vumo and I would not look at one another as we paced and waited. He came out of his meeting grinning, and Nangi nodded sourly at us. He was a believer. I had truly convinced him.

The doubters and hoarders appealed to Wuko the Rain Maker for help. But the Zavaedies in tribehold were still preoccupied with their own problems. The clans of the tribehold broke out into their own pitched battles, each still trying to put forth one of their own daughters as a Vaedi to counter Gladola.

They were useless. We were invincible.

6. *Desperation*

THE PEOPLE FEASTED right up to the day of prophecy. Cagey doubters suddenly switched sides in the last minute, slaughtered their herds and joined us as if they had been believers all along. All the fated day, we spent in celebration.

"I see Sulula!" Sambolo shouted. "What do you see?"

"We see Sulula!" we cried.

"What do you see?"

"We see Sulula!"

"What do you see?"

"We see Sulula!"

Hundreds of beautiful girls danced in Sulula costumes, imitating Gladola. It was quite a sight for me, even if I was not strong enough in my magic to perceive them as anything but gloriously naked. Every married man in the crowd could see Sulula that day, or at least assured his wife that those girls were masked and clothed head to toe.

The sun sank below the horizon. We wore our best clothes, Sulula or not. We held hands and sang songs. We danced without growing exhausted. We were too excited to sleep. The stars above were as bright as ten thousand moons, and the full moon, when it rose, was as bright as a sun. We knew it was a night for magic.

"Do you see the color of the moonlight? Do you see how Sulula it is?" we whispered to each other. Vumo and I grinned together like maniacs. My sister, father, mother, mother's sister, uncle, and my cousin, her husband and their new baby were there too, every-one I loved.

We sang more songs. We waited. The moon set. Dawn rose. Was the sun brighter? Was the light more Sulula? Did we hear the voices of our ancestors upon the hill?

The day stretched.

People began to mutter. Then to complain. Then to shout and argue.

No new cattle appeared, no ancestors joyfully ran to hug us, no granaries overflowed.

The joyful multitude turned into an angry mob. Over and over, I heard the shout, "We have been betrayed!" I may have shouted it myself too. We all felt it. We stormed the homestead of Sambolo, where we demanded an explanation in a thousand voices.

We did not see the Bone Whistler, but we heard the notes of flute music float over us. We calmed enough that Sambolo was able to ap-pear on the flat rooftop of his adobe. He did not inspire confidence. His skin had blanched whiter than bone, he trembled and shrank from the crowd's rage. People began to throw rocks at him. The roar of the mob increased again.

Then the Bone Whistler stepped out. Calm, confident, unafraid. And angry.

"We have been betrayed!" he shouted. We were startled to hear our own grievance flung back at us.

"Yes, betrayed!" he repeated. "What did you expect? While you were sacrificing your last aurochs, what were the fat Zavaedies in the tribehold doing? Do you think they have followed the instructions of the prophecy? They are the worst of all hoarders, and yet we have not stopped them. The ancestors didn't fail us. We failed the ancestors. We flouted their one request, to purify ourselves before they arrived. Is it any wonder they did not appear?"

"What must we do?" Sambolo asked, loudly, for us all to hear.

"Destroy the hoarders," said the Bone Whistler.

❏ ❏ ❏

My brother and I had often wondered why the Bone Whistler did not call for us to take over the tribehold by force much earlier. The day we attacked the tribehold, I finally understood. Even weakened by dissension, even virtually unprotected and taken by surprise, the Rainbow Labyrinth tribehold was the strongest fortress in Faearth. If we had tried to move against the tribehold earlier, too many people would have become discouraged and switched sides again.

Now, however, we had reached the point of no return. We had nothing to eat. Nothing. All the food left in the lands of the Rainbow Labyrinth lay stored up inside the stone maze under the hold. We knew that. We were still fat and strong from months of feasting, but the weeks that followed taught us to fear hunger again.

This was the first battle in which Morvae fought Imorvae, for by now almost all the Imorvae had been purged from our ranks, and Morvae had defected from theirs. The tribehold did not fall easily. Our discipline, edged by desperation, combined with their disorganization, tipped the battle to us. Even then, we might still have lost, but the common people finally threw their lot with us. One moonless night, they opened the gates to us, and by morning the tribehold was ours. Only the guilty were killed. Any one who opposed us was guilty.

7. *Exaltation*

A REPEAT OF THE PREVIOUS MONTHS unfolded now in a matter of mere weeks. Slaughter, feasting, giddy celebration of the new day yet to come. Now *sure* to come. The Bone Whistler opened up the vast storerooms of the subterranean labyrinth under the hold, and we gorged ourselves on it. We learned to vomit between dishes, just to keep eating more. Then we burned the food we could not finish.

We installed the new Vaedi. Gladola and her naked cohort danced through the streets. Every time two people passed and greeted one another, instead of, "Hello, how do you fare?" "Well enough, thank you," one would hear, "Can you see Sulula?" "I see Sulula!"

Sambolo gave a new date for the dawning of the new day: the next full moon.

As Vumo and I burned a pyre of corn, he asked in a voice too low for anyone else to hear, "Vio, what if the new day doesn't come *this* time either?"

This was our terrible dilemma you see. It was too late to back out now. Even if we stopped destroying food, there was not enough left for everyone. We could not replant until next spring. Hundreds would die. The new day was now our only hope.

"It must come," I said. "We mustn't leave a grain left to stop it from coming."

As the orgy of feasting and destruction had repeated, in exaggerated, frenetic repetition, so it was with our last night before the new day.

The word went out. *Everyone* must join. *Everyone* must dance. Not one could stand aside, not if we wanted the new day to dawn. Not if we wanted to see Sulula.

The Bone Whistler played his flute. I had never seen such a mass of people. Everyone who had been spared after the battle, man, woman, child, all pressed into the plaza in the center of the tribe-hold. Though we were all skinny, still there were so many of us, we were pressed flesh to flesh, like rats in a piss ditch.

Sambolo and Gladola led us in the *tama* to bring the new day. It was an unfamiliar dance, clumsy and unlovely. We did not know it. Even the Tavaedies and Zavaedies did not know it. It didn't matter. The Bone Whistler played his flute. For the first time, we felt the true power of that flute. No one could resist the song. There were some who had refused to come to the plaza, but the flute forced them out of their homes and drew them to our ranks. All, *all* of us danced, together, in perfect time. Seven thousand legs lifted as one leg, seven thousand arms lifted as one arm. We were not moving our own limbs, but jerked like puppets to the tune.

It was terrible, it was glorious. Power moved us. It used us, but it also exalted us. I had never been taken out of myself like this before, as if I were no longer a lonely boy, but belonged to a single animal with seven thousand heads and one heart. I felt hope again. This was what had been missing before, this *exaltation*, and I knew, this time, without any more doubt, the new day would come.

All night we danced, limbs on one beast, sure in our faith. And with dawn, the new day...

❑ ❑ ❑

...did not come.

The many-headed beast had danced as one and now it raged as one. We knew we had been betrayed. Who had spoiled the new day *this* time —which doubters, which hoarders? The Bone Whistler had the answer.

He silenced the exhausted crowd, then raised his voice, and magic carried his hiss and thunder to fourteen thousand ears. The Imorvae, he said. They were witches secretly working their own dances to defile the new day. They had been our enemies all along. They had caused the cattle to sicken and die. They had caused all our preparations to fail, our bellies to rumble. They must die.

But hadn't we rid ourselves of the Imorvae?

No. There were yet Imorvae hiding among us, pretending to be Morvae, pretending to be loyal. They were serpents, rats, vermin. We must root them out and exterminate them.

And their leader – oh, the sorrow, the fury, in his face when he revealed this, for this was the worst betrayal of all—their leader was the last one we would expect.

Their leader was Gladola, and her vicious, lying uncle Sambolo.

We acted as one animal. Not a mob, but a predator. Fingers pointed, shrill voices cried out names. Daughters denounced mothers, nephews accused uncles, brothers turned on sisters. The Bone Whistler played his flute and forced all the accused to the center of the plaza, to dance while his warriors tortured them to death. They saved the worst torments for Gladola and Sambolo. The Bone Whistler called for volunteers to help torture them; I stepped forward and he favored me, for he had noticed me by then as one of his most loyal followers.

I would have just beaten them. I didn't know how to prolong pain, but the flute moved through me, and I did things that made them scream. Others helped me. Those two traitors screamed for days. What I did made me feel sick, yet I would have done worse if I could. They had lied to us. Worse, their lies had made many people doubt the new day, doubt Sulula. Doubt the Bone Whistler.

The Persecutions spread. The new day depended on the eradication of the Imorvae, as it depended on the eradication of the hoarders and the doubters. And I saw that this could go on forever, there might always be hidden enemies to drag forward, to explain the delay of the new day. I feared Nangi would eat my thoughts, so I hid my doubts from everyone, even my own brother.

I wanted nothing more than to see the new day dawn. I was to blame for dragging my brother, my father, mother, sister, everyone I loved, into believing in the color I couldn't even see myself. If the new day never dawned, I would not only starve myself, but die with their hunger in my belly too.

This time, we did not wait out the night of the prophecy camped with the multitude. Each family remained at home, isolated, separately begging the ancestors to return to life. Vumo and I sat vigil with five other boys, our sept. We were all of an age to pass the Initiation and test for magic. The Bone Whistler made no secret that he expected us to prove Morvae, and join his cadres of loyal Tavaedies, but who needed Initiation ceremonies when the new day would come tomorrow?

So that night we waited.

We waited.

We waited.

And then everything changed.

❑ ❑ ❑

It's strange, and hard to explain, but I saw it before I believed it: a glow surrounded each of my six companions. I could see a red haze around one boy, orange around another, yellow here, blue there, and purple too. Only my brother had no glow, and only green was missing from the rainbow.

I jumped to my feet like a crazed man. "I see it! Do you see it? I see it! At last I see it! I see Sulula!" Then I jabbed my finger at each boy and called out the color of his glow.

They gaped at me, fish-eyed with shock, for a full minute. Then our sept leader, the biggest and oldest, stood up and shouted.

"Those are not the colors of Sulula! Those are the old colors, and if you see so many, it is because you are Imorvae, and our enemy! It is because of *you* we have not seen Sulula!"

The other boys fell on me, and would have killed me. I was still strong with the colors that moved through me, real magic, fierce and true, and I fought back. I kicked groins, elbowed throats, punched bellies. I broke their limbs and as soon as they fell on their backs, smashed their faces with my bare foot.

I thought they had all tried to kill me, and that I had killed all of them, but one remained. Vumo, my brother, had held back. Now we looked at each other, across a room of our dead friends. My feet were splattered in blood and flecks of brain up to the ankles.

Hate glittered in his eyes, but fear too.

I did not want to kill my brother.

A warrior who had been waiting in another house ran to our door and pushed aside the reed mat. His eyes bugged at what he saw.

"I discovered they were Imorvae," I said. My voice was changing that year, and this came out higher pitched than I liked. But Vumo did not contradict me. The warrior invited us to wait the new day in the other house. I no longer saw anything glow. In fact, I was so tired, I slept.

You know what happened. No new day dawned. We awoke with our hunger.

Have you ever been hungry? I don't mean hungry for a day, for a week. I mean, for months. Each day, you eat a little less. Days go by when you eat nothing at all. Then a bite or two, then days again without. You weaken slowly. Your eyes grow to the size of stomachs, and your stomach grows to the size of an eye.

More hidden Imorvae were found, blamed and killed. A new date was set, the first full moon after the Summer Solstice. Months away. It might as well have been lifetimes. Every night, I wondered if I would wake up to find masked men accusing me of being Imorvae, and every day, when Vumo avoided meeting my eyes, I wondered if my own brother would be the one to turn me in.

Vumo and I kept alive because as part of the army who scourged the land for hoarders, we could steal food. We had the responsibilities of men, though not yet the formal training. It was like that in our army, because so many of the elders had been accused of being Imorvae, or doubters, or hoarders. Ours was an army of the young.

I was given charge of my own sept of men-boys, as was my brother, but this only made things worse between us.

Though we never were formally Initiated, I found I had already earned my Shining Name. The others called me Vio the Skull Stomper, and considered me a great hero because I had killed five "Imorvae." Sometimes, I could bully loose some chops on the strength of my name; other times, I used my fists. Vumo was more sly and less direct, but stole just the same. We quarreled once because he found three sacks of only partly rotted beans and he wasted one of them to bribe some girl to his bed. We quarreled over many things. I asked my warriors to watch him.

For a while, we kept our family alive in this way. But too many other warriors were trying to do the same, most of them outranking us. Hunger narrows your world to your own belly. I spent my days securing crumbs for myself, and Vumo did the same. We didn't share with one another.

Once, I did have enough—a whole bird—I thought of my family for the first time in two moons. I sneaked home.

There was no one in the yard to greet me. My mother and father were dead, sticks so thin even the flies could only land along their limbs in a single file. Their corpses were fresh, though. My nose had become attuned to the subtle scale of foulness of decaying flesh. If I had come only days before, I might have saved them. I could not find my sister.

I searched for her. I found my cousin instead. Her husband had tried to steal food from the Bone Whistler's warriors and died fighting them. And my sister? She said my sister had given herself to a band of warriors. She let them use her in exchange for a basket of grain, which she intended to share with our family. But she was so hungry, she couldn't help herself. She ate all of it and died. Her shrunken stomach burst from the uncooked corn.

"What about you?" I asked. "How did you survive? Where is your baby?"

I will not tell you her reply. It doesn't matter. She died a few weeks later herself.

How much had changed in merely half a year. Once you could walk from one end of our tribal lands to another and stop to feast at every clanhold. Now if you walked the same path, you would see tatters of corpses strewn in front of those same houses. Fields that had been burnt now turned to dust. Billowing storms of dust criss-crossed the whole valley around the tribehold.

Have you ever known guilt? I don't mean feeling guilty over sneaking out to play in the stream for an afternoon when you should have been tending the herd. I don't mean remorse for cheating on your wife. I mean have you ever murdered your own family with your own words, your own foolishness, your own bone-stupid faith in some impossible dream. Have you ever destroyed a whole world and had only yourself to blame. You die slowly from self-hate. You eat away at yourself, until you are nothing left but hard bone under a façade of thin-stretched skin.

The odd thing is, hunger and guilt cancel one another out. A full man has the luxury of suicide. A hungry man is too busy searching for another scrap to eat.

We slaughtered more Imorvae. We were hungry, and they were dead; we had becoming accustomed to staving off famine with desperate feasting. The slaughter of the hidden Imorvae, the last of our enemies, was cause for celebration, but we had no aurochsen left. So we roasted their corpses and feasted. We survived one more day.

Only one eating mat never lacked for food: that of the Bone Whistler. Those warriors he favored would be invited to dance to his flute and then dine with him. It was tiring to dance, but always worth it for the full belly that followed. I was invited several times, while my brother was not, but I knew Vumo could speak a word and bring me down, if I did not denounce him first. On the surface, I was in the stronger position, but I worried. He was crafty. My warriors who spied on my brother reported that he had begun to visit often with Nangi the Thought-Eater.

Summer arrived, full of dust, devoid of rain. Another date approached for the new day—proclaimed by the Bone Whistler himself, and would he lie to us? My brother had been avoiding me, but one evening he sought me out. "I'm going to the piss-pit. Wait a while, then meet me there."

A trap. But I went.

We met in the dark, over the stinking yawn in the ground behind the lodge, pretending to piss. Private meetings were not allowed, not even between brothers, and warriors patrolled everywhere in the Bone Whistler's compound. I could not read Vumo's expression. His face was as dry as a riverbed in a drought.

"Will you sit vigil for the new day with me?" he asked.

"Would you not prefer to wait with Nangi?"

He grinned nervously. I knew from his fear that my suspicions were correct, and he had plotted with her.

"I wish I were like you," he said. "I wish I didn't doubt the new day. I wish I could see Sulula. But if new day doesn't come, I need to look out for myself."

He had a finer face than mine, but I knew my fist was faster. I hefted my stone mace.

He lifted his own weapon, took a skittish step back. "If you know about Nangi, you must know what I have to do."

"Yes." I threw my mace into the ditch and spread my arms. "Do it."

He looked bewildered.

I knelt at the edge of the piss-pit, breathing the filthy vapors. My eyes stung. "Prove your loyalty to the Bone Whistler. But strike the blow yourself. Cull the diseased part of the herd so the good can survive."

My brother stood over me and placed his hands on my head, so gently, in a position to snap my neck.

"What if I *am* the one preventing the new day from dawning?" I whispered. "What if I have to be sacrificed so you can survive? Isn't that worth it?"

He knelt in front of me, his hands on my shoulders. "I'm her *particular* friend."

I didn't understand, but he rushed on.

"I told her she was pretty. I told her I liked her. I told her everything she wanted to believe, so she believed all of it. She can't eat thoughts when her own feelings get in the way." His voice cracked. "Vio, they're all dead. You're all I have left."

On the vigil to wait the new day, my brother decided he would, after all, spend the night with Nangi, his *particular* friend, while I joined the silent crowd of thin men and women in the plaza. To my surprise, I felt a stirring of hope again. I had thought hope dead. Maybe it was. Maybe it was only desperation I felt.

Let it not be too late, I begged the ancestors. *Please come back.* Now I imagined my parents, my sister, my cousin cuddling her baby. *Please come back and say you forgive me.*

Some held hands, but all were silent. We stared at the lightening sky where the sun would rise. And we hoped.

Comments on

"Tomorrow We Dance"

In a novel's equivalent of collage, strands of parallel stories add up to more than the sum of their parts. Each story strand gains something from the way it is placed in between the other story lines. In my fantasy epic series, *The Windwheel and the Maze*, each book has at least three storylines, told from the point of view of one of the major characters, often intertwining past and present. One reader pointed out that the storylines from the past were interesting enough to stand as novellas in their own right. So why not pull out a novella and begin the series with that?

There are two reasons, the same two reasons George Lucus didn't begin the Star Wars Saga with Episode I to III. One, it would give away spoilers for the Empire Strikes Back. ("Luke, I'm your father!" "Duh, dad. Meet my lawyer. You owe me back payments of child support, big time!") The other reason is that those three Star Wars episodes are a tragedy about failure, about how evil, rather than good, triumphs, at a personal and a political level.

That is true of "Tomorrow We Dance" as well.

The main storyline of *The Windwheel and the Maze* follows a traditional heroic arc: the heroine, Dindi, rises from obscurity and powerlessness and learns to wield great power to save the world. The series ends happily. I believe in happy endings, and I believe in the importance of the classic hero mythos, so I do not apologize for revisiting this ground, even if it has been done before. Many coming-of-age stories have been done before, as have many love stories, but if the story is well told, what matters is how *this* child comes of age, how *this* woman and man fall in love, how *this* hero slays the monsters of his own weakness and betters himself.

However, every story of triumph is also a story of failure. Perhaps someone else's failure, but without the contrast, how would we know how bad it could have been if the hero had not triumphed? At a deeper level, the real story *is* the story of failure, because we know that even though the heroine wins, the victory is temporary. Promises of a permanent victory are themselves suspect.

"Tomorrow We Dance" is about a villain, whom Dindi will meet only indirectly in the first book of the series, but later confronts in person, known as Vio the Skull Stomper. This is who he was before he began stomping skulls. There is more to his story, but this is as much as I can tell without revealing spoilers for the rest of the books. (Don't worry, he isn't Dindi's father.) I decided to include this story as a single novelette in this collection because I think it reads differently when read as one piece, not part of the collage. I still intend for it to be interwoven into the *The Windwheel and the Maze*. I hope anyone reading this will want to read the series as well, and not mind too much seeing this part of the story again, seeing how it unfolds transformed by the context of the larger epic.

It took me three years to write this part of the story. It wasn't the writing that took me a long time, but the thinking. I thought it over and over again, and the thought never came out right. How do I show how people abandon their power to a tyrant, how people abandon their reason to madness? Because *The Windwheel and the Maze* is a fairytale, I knew I wanted to do a retelling of *The Pied Pip-*

er and *The Emperor's New Clothes*, rolled into one. But that wasn't enough. I didn't want to just point and laugh at the foolishness of the people taken in by false promises. I wanted to show why *you and I would have danced to the flute too.*

I'm a historian, so I looked to history for help. Finally, I found what I needed when I studied the cattle-killing cult of nineteenth century South Africa. In particular, the non-fiction book *The Dead Will Arise: Nongquawese and the Great Xhosa Cattle-Killing Movement of 1856-7* by J.B. Peires was a tremendous resource for me. It isn't often a non-fiction book makes me cry. Although this story is a fantasy, don't think something like this couldn't happen in real life. It has. Don't think we are so much smarter than those people that something like this couldn't happen again. It could.

Yet just because dreams sometimes die, just because hopes are sometimes false, doesn't mean that it's any better to become a cynic and a skeptic about everything. That's just as dangerous.

At the beginning of the summer of 2010 I had a new baby. Imagine all the cutest LOLcats you've ever seen, and then imagine my baby, who was cuter than that, so it was pretty hard to stay depressed. I threw myself back into writing fiction over the summer. I come up with a million Plans, and they are usually silly, and my family laughs at me, but I had a new Plan.

THE VIRGIN'S CHOICE
(4 OF CUPS)

THE LADY ISAMEIR COULD NOT be matched for her purity, and the proof lay in the fact that her father had used her as bait to capture the King of the Unicorns. She had been shut all her life in a garden at the top of a tower of white sandstone. Her father provided her with fountains tiled in sapphire, pillows of cloth-of-gold, and four magic goblets that would reveal the true nature of those who sipped from them. Yet she wept tears like diamonds when the bronze gate slammed shut behind the unicorn lured into the tower prison by her presence. She stroked his mane and his silky white beard.

"Now you are a prisoner in this tower, as much as I am," she said.

As much as you are, Lady, said the Unicorn King. She looked at him in wonder. He did not speak again.

Three lords courted the Lady in the Tower, drawn by tales of her beauty and her innocence. At her father's behest she invited all three to a banquet that she might choose one to marry.

She served them plates of gold piled with fruits from her garden and pomegranate wine in the magic goblets that revealed a man's true form.

During the feast, each lord boasted of his love for her. However, after they drank, they assumed their true forms.

The first lord began to bleat. He became a ram. Thus Isameir perceived that he had only offered for her because the rest of the herd hailed her as a great trophy.

The second lord began to snort. He became a boar. Isameir perceived that he longed to wallow in her lucre.

The third lord began to crow. He became a rooster. Isameir perceived that he loved her true—for the moment—but by tomorrow, he would love another maiden just as passionately, and leave Isameir's bed empty while he strutted in other henhouses.

She fled the beastly suitors, to the oak at the center of the garden, which grew acorns of solid gold. There she wrapped her arms around the neck of the Unicorn King and wept into his mane.

"How can I choose for my husband a sheep, a pig or a cock?" she asked. She did not expect an answer. Since the day of his capture, though she had poured her heart out to him often, the Unicorn King had only spoken once.

Drink from your goblet, he said, staring into her eyes with his own deep blue pools.

Indeed, she found she still held her goblet in her hand, untouched. She sipped it, then drained it to the dregs. She felt the transformation sweep over her, as her true nature became revealed.

The two unicorns leaped the wall of the tower garden that night, never to return.

Comments on

"The Virgin's Choice"

Tolkien once wrote that fantasy should not be misconstrued as simple allegory. It is rather, imagined history. Yet, history itself is susceptible to turning into an allegory of itself, and how much more so imagined history? This story, one of my Tarot flash fics, veers closer than most to straight allegory. The only thing worse than passing a crass allegory off as a real story would be to interpret it for you....

...but let me just say that in the alchemical work of the occult mystical tradition of neo-platonic and medieval Europe, the Virgin often represented Psyche or the Soul. The soul begins in a state of innocence, but she becomes what she marries. If you marry your soul to something you hold in contempt, eventually, you will hold yourself in contempt. Fiction is a mirror that shows us our true selves, our many possible true selves, and bids us choose.

Over the summer of 2010, I threw myself back into writing fiction. I blogged again. I joined Facebook. Twitter. Etc. (Insert winking, blinking, smiley emoticons here.) I immersed myself in a supportive writing community, where I discovered Indie publishing. I had always associated self-publishing with PublishAmerica typo-fests with atrocious covers, and I had vowed to fall on my own sword rather than come close to it. People whose opinion I respected had warned me not to taint my writing career forever with a self-published book. It was a one-way street, and if I took that route, I could never come back.

I was inspired by the beautiful literary writing of my friend Michelle Davidson Argyle and of Wanda Shapiro; the sassy vampire fiction of Zoe Winters and of Amanda Hocking; and the efforts of heroes in the field, like C.J. Cherryh and Jane Fancher, to keep their backlist on the front shelf by self-publishing. I decided I could do this. If my work had any value to readers, the readers would decide that for themselves. Oh, and if you were sweet enough to be wondering, I also managed to finagle my way back into grad school, at least for the time being.

I realize there is no guarantee of a happy ending. But that's not why you write fiction, or make art, or help the homeless, or try to stop wars, or have babies. That's not why you marry your soul to the pursuit of something pure and beautiful. You do it because you are alive and because you have an obligation to not let the sun go out.

Contact Me

Did you know that if you leave a good review of this book on Amazon or Goodreads you are fifty-seven percent more likely to be reborn as a supermodel or sportscar racer in your next life? I agree, that would suck, but despite the risk, please consider mentioning to all your friends how much you loved this book, or at least, some part of this book. For instance, you could say:"I haven't read anything but the Contact Me blurb at the back, but the book is worth buying just for that."

Questions, comments and fawning praise should be sent to my email: tara@taramayastales.com Complaints should be sent to my agent.

Want to review or blurb a book of mine and read it for free? Just let me know. Are you a writer of science fiction or fantasy with a book coming out that you'd like me to blurb? Just let me know.

Come be my friend on Goodreads, Facebook and Twitter!

And I blog: http://taramayastales.blogspot.com/

www.ingramcontent.com/pod-product-compliance
Lightning Source LLC
Chambersburg PA
CBHW071240130626
46556CB00003B/1088